W9-BRH-768

INSPIRATIONAL ROMANCE

Love Inspired

ISBN-13:978-0-373-87578-8

EAN

LOVE INSPIRED® TITLES AVAILABLE THIS MONTH:

LIATMIFC0210

Love Inspired®

A Match Made in Texas

Arlene James

CHATAM HOUSE

Steeple Hill®

He was jealous!

For the first time in his life, Stephen was actually jealous, and he didn't like it, not one little bit. The question was, what should he do about it?

"Wait, don't go yet, Kaylie. I—I have something to say."

Heart pounding, he held out his hand. She hesitated, but finally drew near, putting her hand in his. A ridiculous smile broke out on his face. It was insane, but he couldn't help a surge of sheer joy.

"I've been unreasonable at times, and I apologize."

"No apology necessary," she told him softly.

"I know it's selfish of me to want to keep you to myself, but it's so much easier when you're here."

"I understand," she said.

"I don't think you do. When you're with me, I feel so…peaceful, hopeful, but it's more than that. It's…"

How could he tell her he had been existing in a barren, lonely place, and Kaylie was his first, perhaps only chance to escape it? She was contentment and peace—and perhaps much too good for the likes of him….

Books by Arlene James

Love Inspired

*The Perfect Wedding
*An Old-Fashioned Love
*A Wife Worth Waiting For
*With Baby in Mind
To Heal a Heart
Deck the Halls
A Family to Share
Butterfly Summer
A Love So Strong
When Love Comes Home
A Mommy in Mind
**His Small-Town Girl
**Her Small-Town Hero
**Their Small-Town Love
†Anna Meets Her Match
†A Match Made in Texas

*Everyday Miracles
**Eden, OK
†Chatam House

ARLENE JAMES

says, "Camp meetings, mission work and church attendance permeate my Oklahoma childhood memories. It was a golden time, which sustains me yet. However, only as a young, widowed mother did I truly begin growing in my personal relationship with the Lord. Through adversity, He has blessed me in countless ways, one of which is a second marriage so loving and romantic it still feels like courtship!"

The author of seventy novels, Arlene James now resides outside Dallas, Texas, with her beloved husband. Her need to write is greater than ever, a fact that frankly amazes her, as she's been at it since the eighth grade! She loves to hear from readers, and can be reached via her Web site at www.arlenejames.com.

A Match Made in Texas
Arlene James

Steeple
Hill®

Published by Steeple Hill Books™

STEEPLE HILL BOOKS

Steeple
Hill®

ISBN-13: 978-0-373-87578-8

Recycling programs
for this product may
not exist in your area.

A MATCH MADE IN TEXAS

www.SteepleHill.com

Printed in U.S.A.

Honor your father and mother—which is the first commandment with a promise—that it may go well with you and that you may enjoy long life on the earth.

—*Ephesians* 6:2-3

To Susan (aka Janis Susan May),
my sister in so many ways that
we were almost surely separated at birth!
Love,
DAR

Chapter One

She couldn't help being impressed. As a nurse, Kaylie Chatam had encountered many patients whose physical conditions sadly diminished them, but not this time. Not even the bulk of the casts protecting his broken bones deflected attention from the big, commanding presence asleep on the high, half tester bed. Tall and long-limbed yet brawny, with an air of intensity about him even in sleep that his shaggy blond hair and lean, chiseled face did nothing to diminish, he emitted a potent force, a larger-than-life aura.

Kaylie lifted a petite hand to the heavy, sandy-red chignon at the nape of her neck, wishing that she'd secured it more firmly that morning when dressing for church. She'd have preferred to conduct this interview in the shapeless scrubs that she always wore when working, her long, straight hair scraped back into a tight knot. Instead, here she stood, wearing skimpy flat mules with big silver buckles on the shallow toes, a straight knee-length skirt and a frothy confection of a white blouse, her hair slipping and sliding, tendrils hanging about her face.

Turning to the man crowded next to her in the doorway of the bedchamber in one of the second-floor suites of Chatam

House, the antebellum mansion owned by her three delightful aunties, Kaylie felt at a distinct disadvantage. Stocky, blunt-featured and of medium height with short, prematurely gray hair, a practiced smile and a pricey, light grayish brown suit, Aaron Doolin had identified himself as the patient's agent.

"Who is he exactly?"

"Who *is* he?" Doolin parroted, obviously shocked. "Who *is* he? Why, that's the Hangman." At her blank look, he went on. "Stephen Gallow. Starting goalie for the Fort Worth Blades hockey team." He glanced at the bed, muttering, "At least he was before the accident."

A hockey goalie? Here at Chatam House? She knew little about the game beyond its reputation for violence, but that was enough to make her wonder what the aunties had gotten themselves into now. More to the point, what had they gotten *her* into? Provided, of course, that she decided to take on this patient, which she could not do in good conscience without at least nominal approval from her father.

"What happened to the bed hangings?" she asked Doolin, gesturing toward the massive headboard of the bed. One of her aunts' prized English antiques, it stood a good seven feet in height. Even the square footposts were taller than Kaylie, though at a mere five feet in her stocking feet, that wasn't saying too much.

Doolin just shrugged. "I don't know from hangings."

"The curtains at the sides of the front of the bed."

"Oh!" He waved a hand, the sapphire on his pinky flashing in the midday light. The edges of his ever-present smile frayed. "Well, during the excitement last night—" he churned his hands then shrugged sheepishly "—they sort of came down in the scrum. Your aunts thought it best to get them out of the way."

Kaylie analyzed that and came to the conclusion that whatever had happened the night before had involved a certain amount of violence, which explained why the original nurse had walked out and why she was here at Chatam House, staring at an injured, sleeping *hockey player.* The idea still did not quite compute. She tilted her head and wondered what was so compelling about this particular patient.

That he was handsome could not be denied, despite the faint slanting scars on his chin and high on his right cheek. Thick, pale gold hair formed a shaggy frame for a rectangular face with large, even features, the eyes set deeply beneath the slashes of incongruently dark brows. The sooty shadow of a beard that hadn't seen a razor in some days colored his square jaws, cheeks and chin, calling attention to wide, surprisingly soft lips that might have looked feminine in a less aggressively masculine face.

How was she, a pediatric nurse, supposed to deal with a man like this?

Kaylie almost turned around and walked away right then, but her aunts would not have asked this of her if the need were not acute. They had approached Kaylie immediately after worship service that morning, asking her to stop by the mansion at her earliest opportunity. Some tinge of desperation in that request had made Kaylie drop off her father at his—*their*—house and drive straight here. Only then had she learned of the aunts' guest and his need for nursing care. She had been shocked, to say the least.

Known for their good works, the Chatam sisters, triplets in their seventies, often opened their historic antebellum mansion to family and family connections, but this was the first time in Kaylie's memory that they had ever taken in a complete stranger. His situation must be desperate, indeed. She turned to Aaron Doolin once more.

"What is his condition?"

"Drugged," he replied flippantly.

Kaylie just looked at the man. Of course Gallow was drugged. Obviously so. It was nearly one o'clock in the afternoon, and the man was sleeping as soundly as if two people were not standing in his room talking. She understood that the doctor had been called in during the night to sedate the patient. Such a heavy dose indicated that the poor man had been in great physical distress.

Doolin cleared his throat and got serious. "You want to know about his injuries. Uh, let's see. Stevie broke his leg and arm. The arm was pretty bad. That and the ribs is why they've strapped it to his chest that way, and naturally it had to be his left arm because he is left-handed." Doolin grinned and added proudly, "One of the few truly left-handed goalies in the league."

"Is that good?"

The agent goggled at her. "Good?" Shaking his head at her obvious ignorance of all things hockey, he sent her a pitying look. "That, Miss Chatam, is a very good thing, indeed. Especially if said lefty is a big brute with reflexes quick as a cat and the eyesight of an eagle."

A brute. His own agent called him a brute. She could just imagine how her father, a retired pastor, would feel about that. Hub Chatam considered his youngest son's participation in pro rodeo barbaric. Chatam men, he asserted firmly and often, were called to higher purposes than mere sport. Chatam men were lawyers and pastors, doctors and professors, bankers and titans of industry who used their wealth and talents for the good of others in the name of Christ. That Chandler chose to dismiss his father's convictions was a great bone of contention within the family. No doubt, Hub would hold an even less favorable opinion of a pro hockey player, though of course a boarder and patient wasn't the same thing as a son.

"Sorry," she muttered to the agent. "Not much of a sports fan. My field is medicine."

"Medicine. Right. Gotcha. About his condition... Let's see... Broken bones. Two in the right leg, two in the left arm, four ribs, collarbone. I think that's it. Internally, there was a lacerated liver, a bruised pancreas, busted spleen..." Doolin tsked and shook his head. "I don't know what all."

Kaylie nodded in understanding. "Concussion?"

"Um, unofficially, he got conked pretty good."

Unofficially? "Was there brain damage?"

Aaron Doolin reared back. "No way! He's sharp as ever!" The agent smiled. "Mouth certainly works. He's singeing my ears regular again, but hey, that's what I get paid for. Right?" He chuckled, only to sober when it became obvious that she wouldn't join in with anything more than a weak smile.

Stephen Gallow sounded like both a brute and a bully, but who was she to judge such things? Her one concern should be the health of the patient. "What about his lungs?" she asked. "Were they punctured?"

"Nothing said about it."

"They would have mentioned something like that," Kaylie told him. "Trust me."

Nodding, Aaron looked to the bed. "Kid's got plenty to deal with as it is."

No doubt about that, Kaylie mused, thinking of her father, who had suffered a heart attack some six months earlier. Compared to all this man had been through, that seemed almost minor, though Hub continued to behave as if his life remained in immediate danger. She wandered closer to the bed.

Stephen Gallow moaned and twitched, muttering what sounded like, "Nig-nig."

Doolin slid his hands into his pants pockets. "Must think he's talking to Nick."

"Nick? Who's that?"

"Uh, old buddy."

"He's dreaming, then."

"Yeah, yeah. Does a lot of that since the accident." Doolin churned his hands again, in what seemed to be a habitual gesture. "The trauma of it all, I guess."

"He's suffered some very serious injuries," Kaylie murmured.

"You're telling me! Man, I thought he'd bought it, you know?"

"How long ago was the accident?"

"Nine, ten days." He looked at his client, and for the first time the mask of beaming bonhomie slipped, showing genuine concern. "Ask me, he oughta be in the hospital still."

Kaylie smiled to herself. Patients and family were often of that opinion, but home could be a safer, more restful environment than the hospital.

"But you know how it is," Doolin went on. "A big sports star draws attention that hospitals don't particularly appreciate, and when said sports star is trying to keep a low profile... Well, that's why we're here, obviously."

Kaylie furrowed her brow at that. "You mean he's hiding out here at Chatam House?"

The agent licked his lips warily before admitting, "You could say that."

"From who?"

"The press, mostly."

"But why Chatam House? How did he wind up here?"

"Oh, that." The pinky ring flashed again. "Brooksy arranged it."

Brooksy? "You mean Brooks Leland? *Doctor* Brooks Leland?"

Doolin's gray head bobbed. "Yeah, yeah. Me and Brooksy, we went to college together. We were fraternity brothers, and hey, once a frat bro, always a frat bro. Right?"

Frat bro. A smile wiggled across Kaylie's lips. She'd

remember that and give her older brother's best friend—that was, *Brooksy*—a hard time about it later. Obviously, Doolin had called Brooks about his patient's need to keep a low profile while recovering from his accident and Brooks had contacted the aunts, apparently Aunt Odelia specifically. Finally, this situation was beginning to make some sort of sense.

"So what do you think?" Aaron Doolin asked. "Can you do it? He just mainly needs someone to help him get around and manage his pain, meds and meals." He eyed her warily. "You think you can make him take his medicine?"

Make him? Kaylie lifted a slender eyebrow at that. She thought of her father again. At seventy-six, Hub Chatam was twice widowed and a retired minister. As the youngest of his four children and the only daughter, she'd taken a leave of absence from her job after his heart attack in order to move into his house, take care of him and help him adjust to the new lifestyle necessitated by his health realities. Six months later, he still wouldn't take a pill that didn't come from her hand. He claimed that he couldn't keep them straight, but let ten minutes pass the appointed time for one of his meds and he was demanding to know when she was going to dispense it.

Before she could answer the agent's question, Gallow's eyes popped open. Startled by their paleness—they were like marbles of gray ice—Kaylie registered the panic in them. She instinctively started forward just a heartbeat before he bolted up into a sitting position. Roaring in pain, he dropped back onto the pillow. A blue streak of profanity rent the air, then he gasped and began to writhe.

Though taken aback, Kaylie instantly realized that he was doing himself damage. Stepping up to his bedside, she bent over him and calmly advised, "Be still. Take slow breaths. Slow, shallow breaths." For the first time he looked at her. Confusion, anger and pain poured out of those eerily pale eyes, but as he stopped moving and gradually controlled his breathing, lucidity took hold of him. Impulsively, Kaylie brushed a pale gold lock from his brow, smiling encouragingly. "Slow…slow… That's it."

His pale gaze skimmed over her with acute curiosity even as he followed her instructions. After a moment, he swallowed and rasped, "Who are you?"

"Kaylie Chatam. Hypatia, Odelia and Magnolia Chatam are my aunts."

"Kaylie's a nurse," Aaron Doolin put in helpfully. "How about that? The old biddies, er, our *hostesses* had one in the family. Go figure."

Gallow's gaze abruptly shifted to his agent. Kaylie shivered. Had she been the recipient of that suddenly furious, frigid, accusatory glare, she'd have ducked. Doolin just ratcheted up his grin and spread his hands.

"Hey, Stevie! That's my boy. How you feeling there, huh?"

"How do you think I feel?" Gallow gritted out. "And don't call me Stevie."

"Sure. Sure. Doc says you reinjured those ribs last night. Must be killing you."

Literally baring his teeth, Gallow revealed a pair of spaces on the right side where his upper and lower second molars should be. Something about those empty spaces pricked Kaylie's heart. He was no longer the impossibly handsome sports figure or the angry brute but a mere man at the mercy of his own injuries. Until he snarled.

"Reinjured my ribs? You think? That ba—" He slid a gaze over Kaylie. "That bozo ball of lard you hired to take care of me threw himself on top of me! *That's* what reinjured my ribs."

Doolin lifted his hands as if to ward off a blow. "Hey, calm down, will you? How was I to know the guy would do that? I mean, he's a nurse, right? He said you were all over the place and that he was trying to pin you down so you wouldn't fall off the bed."

"He was trying to pin me down, all right, and enjoyed every second of it, until I kicked him in the—" Gallow broke off there and gave Kaylie an irritated look.

Doolin chuckled. "You gave him an anatomy lesson he didn't get in nursing school, that's for sure."

Kaylie stepped back and folded her arms, appalled. This man was a powerhouse of lithe physical strength and jagged emotion that ranged far beyond her personal experience. Stephen Gallow sent her a cool, challenging look. She felt frozen and singed at the same time. A sense of foreboding shivered through her as she watched him take his agent to task with little more than a glare and growl.

"Where's the bozo now?"

"Fired him last night."

"And you think he's going to keep his mouth shut after this?"

"He signed a nondisclosure, and I sent the attorney to remind him of that in person this morning, along with a check for his trouble."

In other words, Kaylie thought, shocked, *they'd paid off the man!* Whether to keep him quiet or forestall a lawsuit, she didn't know. Most likely both. Obviously she had stumbled into a situation that was well beyond her depth.

Gallow dropped his eyelids, his right hand sliding lightly over his left side. Kaylie could tell that he was still in great pain, and the nurse in her could not stand by and watch it, no matter how rough and tough a character he might be. She looked to Doolin.

"Where is his pain medication?"

The agent reached into his coat pocket and drew out a prescription bottle. "Brooks says anything stronger has to be given by injection, and that requires a professional," Doolin said pointedly. "Until we hire another nurse, this is the best we can do."

She took the bottle and read the prescription before going to the bedside table, where a crystal pitcher of water and matching glass stood. She poured water into the glass, uncapped the pill bottle and shook two huge tablets into her palm.

"These should give you some relief, but you'll have to sit up to take them. Will you let me help you?"

Gallow ignored her, demanding of Doolin, "What have you told her?"

Aaron shrugged. "Just what she needs to know."

"Will you let me help you?" Kaylie repeated.

Gallow slid her a dismissive glance. "I don't like being knocked out all the time."

"Taking the meds regularly is the best way to prevent that. Regular doses will keep your pain under control while allowing you to gradually build up a resistance to the narcotic effect. Take them irregularly and they'll knock you out every time."

He glared at her for a moment, but then he held his breath and slowly pushed up onto his right elbow. Kaylie quickly pressed the first tablet between his lips and lifted the glass. He gulped, tilted his head back and swallowed. They repeated the process with the second tablet before he collapsed once more upon the pillow, panting slightly.

Kaylie heard his stomach rumble. Setting aside the glass, she began to reposition the pillow and smooth the covers, trying to make him comfortable until the medication kicked in. As she worked, she spoke briskly to Doolin.

"Please go down and ask my aunts to have Hilda prepare a breakfast tray."

"Okay. Sure. But I thought the staff had the day off."

"They do, but she'll fix something anyway." The aunties

took care of their own meals on Sundays, but Hilda had always been a compassionate woman.

Kaylie smoothed the covers over Stephen Gallow's feet with gentle hands. They were enormous feet. Not even Chandler had feet the size of these. She tried to imagine the size of the skates that he would need.

Stephen rumbled out an order. "Coffee."

"Oh, that may not be possible," Kaylie interjected apologetically. "My aunts don't drink coffee, but maybe they'll have some in the kitchen anyway."

Gallow grimaced as Aaron scuttled out of the room. Kaylie told herself that she had done all she could for the moment. It was time to go. And yet, she lingered, oddly reluctant to leave the injured man alone. Brute he might be, but to a nurse an injured man was an injured man. Period. At least that's what she told herself.

As soon as Aaron had gone, Kaylie Chatam started tidying up the place. Stephen had dropped a towel on the floor the evening before, along with a trio of little pillows that had decorated the bed. Too weak to retrieve them, he'd simply left them where they'd fallen and collapsed, exhausted after the drive from Dallas, the climb up the stairs and a cursory scrubbing. Nurse Chatam folded the towel and laid it atop the upholstered bench at the foot of the bed. The pillows she moved to one of a pair of window seats with gold-on-gold-striped upholstery, both of which overlooked the front of the house. Stephen followed her every movement with his wary gaze.

Petite and gentle, with big, dark brown eyes and thick, straight hair a shade somewhere between sandy brown and red, she was pretty in a painfully wholesome way. That put her a far cry from his usual type, beautiful and somewhat flamboyant. After all, if a guy was going to put up with all that female nonsense, Stephen figured that he ought to get something flashy out of it, something noticeable.

This Kaylie Chatam didn't even appear to be wearing makeup, except perhaps mascara, as her lashes were much darker than her delicate brows, and a touch of rose-pink lipstick. He couldn't help noticing, however, that the creamy skin of her slender oval face seemed almost luminous with good health. He noted that she shared with her aunts a high forehead and faintly cleft chin. That little dip in her almost pointy chin somehow called attention to the plump, rosy lips above, not to mention those enormous eyes. They were so dark they were almost black, startlingly so with her light hair. He wondered just how long her hair was and what she'd do if he managed to pluck the pins from that loose, heavy knot at the nape of her slender neck. More to distract himself from that line of thought than for any other reason, he broke the silence.

"Aaron explain about the press?"

"He said you're hiding from them."

"I'm not hiding!" Stephen frowned at the notion. "I'm keeping a low profile."

"Ah."

"It's necessary," he grumbled defensively, rubbing his right hand over his prickly jaw and chin and wishing he could shave. "You wouldn't understand."

"No, I guess not."

Something about those softly spoken words irritated him, and he barked at her. "Your aunts swore they would protect my privacy, and I made a hefty contribution to some single parents' charity to guarantee it."

She gave him a look, the kind she might give a little boy who stretched the truth. It made his cheeks and throat heat. He mentally winced at the thought of the curse words that he'd spewed earlier.

"My aunts never swear," she told him with the absolute authority of one who would know. "But if they said they would protect your privacy, then they will. And any donation you may have made to one of their charities has nothing to do with it. Trust me. They may have promised, but they didn't swear."

"What's the difference?" he wanted to know, sounding grumpy even to his own ears.

"'But I tell you,'" she quoted softly, "'Do not swear at all: either by heaven, for it is God's throne; or by the earth, for it is His footstool; or by Jerusalem, for it is the city of the Great King.'"

Stephen gaped at her. Had she just quoted the Bible to him?

"It's from Matthew, chapter five, verses thirty-four and thirty-five."

She had quoted the Bible to him!

"So what are you," he demanded, scowling, "some kind of religious nut?"

Folding her small, delicate hands, she regarded him serenely. "Yes, I suppose you could say that, if 'religious nut' is code for Christian."

Realizing that he'd insulted her, he deepened his frown, muttering, "No offense."

"None taken," she replied lightly, smiling that smile again.

He had the distinct impression that she felt sorry for him and that it had nothing to do with his physical condition.

"Guess your aunts are religious, too?"

"Yes, of course."

Disconcerted, he said nothing more on the subject, just lay there frowning at her. What on earth, he wondered sourly, had he gotten himself into now?

Aaron had touted Chatam House as a bona fide mansion, a posh throwback to an age of bygone opulence, owned and maintained by three dotty old maids with more money than sense, a trio of do-gooders so far out of the loop that they wouldn't know a juicy news item if it bit them. He had seemed right on the money, going by yesterday's brief impressions. In truth, Stephen had been so exhausted and in such pain from the nearly fifty-mile trip from the Dallas hospital down to the smaller city of Buffalo Creek in Aaron's luxury sedan that he'd barely registered the old ladies' names or faces. Before making the laborious climb up the curving staircase behind Chester, their balding butler, they had informed him that he was to be installed in the "small suite," so called because the sitting room was the smallest in the house.

Stephen supposed Chatam House was opulent enough, provided one admired antiques and crystal chandeliers, but he missed his own place and especially his spacious private bath, complete with sauna, walk-in shower, television and music system. This room didn't even have a closet, for pity's sake, just an enormous antique wardrobe, not that he had many clothes with him, just baggy shorts and sweatpants and cut-up T-shirts to accommodate his injuries. Now he learned that he'd landed smack-dab in the middle of a pack of "*godsdienstige ijveraars*," as his stepfather would say, otherwise known as "religious zealots."

Stephen had been acquainted with other Christians, of course, his American grandmother, for one. She'd died after his parents had divorced when he was eight and his mother had taken him back to Holland with her to live. Some of his friends back in Groningen, where they had lived with his mother's parents before her remarriage, had been professing Christians, but they'd never talked about it much. Even some of the guys on the hockey team were Christians, but none of them had ever gone so far as to quote the Bible to him! The most any of them had done was invite him to church, though he'd never gone.

He had enough problems now without finding that he'd landed in the midst of a bunch of religious eccentrics. In fact, he'd say that the very last thing he needed right now was to land in the midst of a bunch of religious eccentrics.

The thing was, he didn't have anywhere else to go. Any hotel large enough to accommodate his needs would also leave him open to the sharp eyes of the press. He had considered convalescing at Aaron's house, but that, too, was under constant surveillance by the local sportswriters. Plus, Stephen couldn't quite bring himself to impose on the newlyweds. Chatam House had seemed like the answer, with Buffalo Creek being close enough to allow Aaron easy access but far enough from the Dallas/Fort Worth Metroplex area to keep the press off his scent.

At this point, his only hope was that the press would not make a big deal of the circumstances of the accident that had knocked him out of the playoffs so that management of the Blades hockey team would not feel duty-bound to activate the good conduct clause of his contract and cut him from the team.

That alone would keep him where he was here in Chatam House, *godsdienstige ijveraars* or not.

Chapter Two

Kaylie Chatam walked around the bed and gathered up the other pillow, saying, "You'll need to sit up a bit in order to eat."

"Yeah, yeah," Stephen muttered on a sigh, grateful for something to think about besides his predicament. He began struggling up onto his right elbow again.

Kaylie swiftly moved back around the bed, her flats slapping lightly against the gleaming hardwood floor. She reached his side and wedged the pillow beneath his head and shoulders, but it still wasn't enough to allow him to eat without decorating himself with his food.

"Let me help you move up on the pillows a little more."

Leaning across him, she slid her hands into the crevices between his torso and arms. He was surprised at the wiry strength that allowed her to actually be of help. After he got settled again, she briskly straightened his T-shirt so that it didn't bind his shoulders and neck. Next, she spread the towel across his chest. Embarrassed by his helplessness, Stephen mumbled, "Thank you."

"You're welcome."

Her soft, rather husky voice sent an odd shiver through him.

"Would you like for me to examine your incisions?"

He shook his head, his right hand going to the spot on his right side where they'd opened him up. "The doctor took a look last night. Said everything seemed fine."

Nodding, she seemed to cast about the room for something more to do. Stephen's gaze followed her.

Despite the lack of certain amenities, he decided that this was really a very elegant room. The cool creams and warm golds, set against a milky brown background, showed off the expensive antiques, rich brocades and matching stripes to perfection.

From where he lay, he could look straight through the open doorway to the gracefully proportioned, brown velvet sofa, placed squarely in the center of a large, truly beautiful cream-on-gold rug positioned in front of an ornate plastered fire-place. He recalled an armchair upholstered in striped satin and a writing desk of some sort, as well as crystal lamps and gold-framed paintings.

It was all a little Victorian for his personal taste, but he couldn't deny the beauty of it. His own home was as sleek and modern as it was possible to be, all shiny blacks and bright colors. It seemed rather cold and pedestrian in comparison. Maybe he ought to rethink that. Be easy enough to make some changes while they were rebuilding the place. Just the thought of what had to be done to make his house on the west side of Fort Worth habitable again—and how it had come to be in need of repair—pained and exhausted him, so he shoved it out of mind.

Thankfully, Aaron returned just then with a laden tray, an-nouncing gaily, "Hey, they got a dumbwaiter. Imagine that. Comes up out there on the landing. It's like an elevator for food, but Hilda says she sends the laundry up that way, too. Pretty slick, huh?"

Stephen nodded and shrugged. "There's one in my stepfather's flat in Amsterdam, where the houses are very old. It works on a pulley."

Kaylie took the tray and placed it on Stephen's lap, asking, "Older than this place? Chatam House is almost a hundred and fifty years old, you know."

He smirked at this. "My stepfather's flat is in a converted *herenhuis* built in 1632."

She blinked. "My, that is old."

"Sixty percent of the houses in Amsterdam were built before the eighteenth century," he muttered, mentally cataloging the contents of the tray. He identified orange juice; eggs scrambled with parsley and diced onion; toast with butter and strawberry jelly; four slices of crisp bacon; a baked apple sprinkled with cinnamon and swimming in cream; and what appeared to be a cup of strong black coffee.

"Mmm," he said, inhaling appreciatively.

Kaylie smiled. "You'll find the fare at Chatam House on an entirely different plane than that of most hospital food."

"No kidding."

He picked up the ridiculously delicate china cup from its matching saucer and touched it to his lips for a quick sample, then made a face. Hot tea. Yuck. He'd never developed a taste for it, and his mother had not pressed him to. He set the cup back onto the saucer and reached for the orange juice instead.

Kaylie chuckled and said to Aaron, "There's a chain coffee shop down on North Main, about a block south of the highway. They have a drive-through window, but I'm sure that if you pick up his favorite grind, Hilda will be happy to make it for him."

"All right," Aaron said, digging into his pocket for his keys. "Be right back."

"I have to be going, too," Kaylie said, swinging toward the door.

Both Aaron and Stephen spoke at the same time.

"What?"

"Where are you going?"

"Home," she answered, turning to face them.

"B-but what about Steve?" Aaron asked, waving a hand toward the bed.

"I don't know. Who stayed with him last night after you fired the nurse?"

"I did," Aaron answered.

"Well, then…"

"I've got a brand-new wife at home!" he exclaimed, twisting to throw Stephen a pleading look.

Kaylie's eyebrows rose at that, but she said only, "I'm sorry, but I'm not prepared to stay at this point. Aren't there any family—"

"None close," Stephen interrupted tersely, frowning.

"Mom's in Holland," Aaron explained. "Dad's in Lubbock. No siblings."

"Friends?"

Stephen sighed richly. Yeah, like his hard-partying friends would take turns sitting at his bedside. Besides, the team was busy. This was their first year to make the playoffs, and the last thing he wanted was to become more of a distraction to them than he already was.

Aaron rubbed his chin. "Cherie, maybe."

"Who's Cherie?" Kaylie asked.

Aaron waved a hand. "Aw, that's Stephen's girlfriend-of-the-moment."

"Aaron," Stephen scolded, glaring a warning that his agent completely missed.

"The female du jour," the social lummox blathered on, "flavor of the month. Matter of fact, unlike you, she's a not-so-natural red—"

"Aaron!" Stephen shouted forcefully enough that Aaron actually closed his mouth. Finally. Stephen muttered, "Cherie's just a team secretary." A team secretary who liked to style herself as his girlfriend whenever it seemed convenient for her.

A shop-made redhead, with a store-bought figure and trendy "bee-stung" lips, the only things real about Cherie were her hands and feet. Even her fingernails and eyelashes were fake, not to mention her cheekbones and chin. That penchant for plastic surgery and high-end beauty salons hadn't seemed like any big deal to Stephen; now it suddenly seemed a little…tawdry, and he didn't want her anywhere near the Chatams. Truth to tell, he didn't want her near, period. He just didn't have the energy to play her game right now.

"Ah. Well, someone's going to have to bring him his supper. We've already imposed on Hilda enough for one Sunday," Kaylie was saying to Aaron. "After he's eaten, if you just make him comfortable, he should sleep through until morning."

"But what about the night?" Aaron began. "Someone has to be here in case he hurts himself again."

"If she doesn't want to help us, she doesn't want to help us!" Stephen barked.

"I didn't say that," Kaylie insisted. "It's just not a decision I can make instantly."

Aaron sighed, shoulders slumping. "Okay, okay. I'll sack out in the other room."

"Don't strain yourself," Stephen muttered, picking up a heavy silver fork and attacking his eggs with his right hand.

"Stevie," Aaron said placatingly, "it's not me. It's Dora."

Aaron's bride of some three months was given to pouting if Aaron neglected her, which, Stephen admitted silently, happened too often. Still, what was he supposed to do without help? Didn't the small fortune that he paid Aaron count for something?

Kaylie stepped backward. "Well, I'll leave you to your meal."

"But you'll let us know about the job soon, right?" Aaron pressed.

"I'll let you know tomorrow."

She whirled and hurried away. Stephen dropped his fork and fixed his agent—and, in truth, his friend—with a glare.

"Now what?" he demanded, suddenly weary again. For once, Aaron had no glib response. "That's what I thought," Stephen muttered morosely.

Hurrying down the gracefully curving marble staircase, her hand skimming the gleaming dark wood of the banister, Kaylie pondered the situation. Stephen Gallow was unlike any man she'd ever encountered. She wasn't at all sure, frankly, that she liked him, but her like or dislike was not the issue. Part brute and part little boy, he presented a problem: she didn't quite know how to deal with him. How could she? The men in her life were calm, solid, accomplished, erudite, polite...in short, gentlemanly.

Her father, Hubner Chandler Chatam, Jr., was a retired minister. Bayard, her eldest brother by more than three decades, was a banker, and Morgan, at forty-two, a history professor. Even her third brother, Hubner Chandler Chatam III—known as Chandler or Chan and twenty-nine to her twenty-four—had a degree in agricultural engineering, though to her father's disgust, he made his living mainly in pro rodeo competition. Of all the men she knew, Kaylie supposed that Chandler had most in common with Stephen Gallow, but he never snarled, lost his temper, behaved rudely or, God forbid, cursed. At least, not as far as she knew. And Chandler was a believer, a Christian. Stephen Gallow was obviously not.

Moreover, Gallow was a little crude, or as her father would put it, rough as a cob, though not lacking in all sensibility. He had moderated his language, with some difficulty, on her behalf. None of that, however, changed the fact that he had been gravely injured. He needed help. He needed a nurse. He needed her—far more than her father did, certainly, which made her wonder if this was God's way of showing Hubner Chatam that his life was not over.

It was not time for Hub to stop living, and so, in her opinion, it was not time for him to stop ministering. The man whose spiritual strength had for so long guided countless others had somehow gotten lost in his own physical and emotional pain, and though her heart went out to him, Kaylie knew that she had to somehow help him find his way again. Was that God's purpose in bringing Stephen Gallow into their lives? Would Gallow's condition and her attention to him help Hub realize that he should and could reclaim his own life?

She paused in the grand foyer at the foot of the stairs to gaze through the window at the side of the bright yellow door with its formal black trim to the boxy little red convertible that was her one extravagance in life. It was the only thing she had not given up when she'd quit her job and moved from her apartment into her father's house to care for him after his heart attack. She'd sold every stick of furniture that she'd accumulated in her twenty-four years, such as it was, and even gotten rid of the contents of her kitchen because the one in her father's small, two-bedroom frame house did not have room for her things. At the time, she'd told herself that it was necessary. Now, with Hub constantly comparing her to her aunts, who had cared for their own widowed father until his death at the age of ninety-two, she feared that she had made a big mistake.

Lately, as if sensing her dissatisfaction with the situation, Hub had taken to regularly remarking that not all of God's children were called to marriage, implying that she had been called to follow in the footsteps of her maiden aunts. He even quoted Paul on the subject, choosing selected verses from I Corinthians 7. Kaylie had heard them so often that she could recite them from memory.

Now to the unmarried and the widows I say: It is good for them to stay unmarried.... An unmarried woman or virgin is concerned about the Lord's affairs: Her aim is to be devoted to the Lord in both body and spirit...

But hadn't Paul also said that every man should have his own wife and every wife her own husband, that man should leave his parents and cleave unto his wife?

Kaylie shook her head. She knew that Scripture did not contradict itself, that it only appeared to when certain verses were taken out of context, but that did not help her determine what God intended for her specifically. She had dated little, too caught up in school and the demands of her family, faith and career to pay much attention to anything else, but she'd always assumed that one day she would marry and have children. Then two years ago, her mother had died at the age of fifty-six after a brief bout with cancer, and six months ago her twice-widowed father had suffered a massive heart attack. Kaylie's father and three older brothers had all assumed that Kaylie would drop everything and take over Hubner's care. So she had.

Now, she feared that had been a mistake for both her and her father. Perhaps God's answer to that dilemma occupied the half tester bed upstairs. Unless presented very carefully, however, her father would see this job as her abandoning him. She did not wish to deceive or disrespect him, of course. He was her father, after all. She certainly did not want to go against his express wishes, but if God willed that she take this job, then she must. The question was, what did God will in this matter?

Kaylie heard the clink of a silver spoon stirring tea in a

china cup. The aunties would be in the front parlor, taking tea after their lunch. The aunties "ate simple" on Sundays, so that the staff could have the day off, just as God commanded, but that did not keep them from indulging in their one great mutual joy: a hot cup of tea. Their parents, Hubner, Sr. and Augusta Ebenezer Chatam, had spent their honeymoon of several months duration in England back in 1932, returning as staunch Anglophiles, with a shipload of antiques and a mutual devotion to tea. They had passed on that passion to their eldest daughters.

Just the thought of her aunts made Kaylie smile. They were darlings, all three of them, each in her own inimitable fashion.

Kaylie turned and walked across the golden marble floor of the foyer toward the front parlor. The aunts called out an effusive welcome as she entered the room.

Though chock-full of antiques, Tiffany lamps, valuable bric-a-brac and large, beautiful flower arrangements, the parlor was a spacious chamber with a large, ornately plastered fireplace set against a wall of large, framed mirrors, including one over the mantel that faced the foyer door. The aunts sat gathered around a low, oblong piecrust table, its intricate doilies hidden beneath an elaborate tray covered with Limoges china. Odelia and Magnolia sat side by side on the Chesterfield settee that Grandmother Augusta had brought back from her honeymoon trip, while Hypatia occupied one of a pair of high-backed Victorian armchairs upholstered in butter-yellow silk.

Though triplets, they were anything but identical personality-wise. Hypatia had been the reigning belle of Buffalo Creek society in her day, as elegant and regal as royalty. It was largely thanks to her that Chatam House had endured into the twenty-first century and adapted to the modern era with its dignity and graceful ambience intact. That she had never married, or even apparently come close to doing so, puzzled all five of her siblings, including her unmarried sisters.

Magnolia, on the other hand, had never evinced the slightest interest in romance, at least according to Kaylie's father Hub, Jr., their older brother. Mags had a passion for growing things and spent hours daily in her cavernous greenhouse out back. A tomboy as a girl, she still had little patience with the feminine frills that so entranced her sister Odelia.

Secretly, Kaylie was most fond of Odelia, who was affectionately known by the vast coterie of Chatam nieces and nephews as Auntie Od. With her silly outfits and outlandish jewelry, she always provided a chuckle, but it was her sweet, softhearted, optimistic, almost dreamy approach to life that made her the epitome of Christian love in Kaylie's mind. Odelia also seemed to be the only one of the sisters who had ever come close to marriage.

"Kaylie, dear, how is the patient?" Hypatia wanted to know as soon as Kaylie sank down upon the chair opposite her.

"Handsome, isn't he?" Odelia piped up. She'd still wore her Sunday best, a white shirtwaist dotted with pink polka dots. The dots easily measured two inches in diameter, as did the faceted, bright pink balls clipped to her earlobes. Her lipstick mimicked the pink of her dress, creating a somewhat startling display against the backdrop of her pale, plump face and stark white, softly curling hair. Like her sisters and the majority of the Chatams, including Kaylie herself, she had the cleft in her chin.

Kaylie chose to answer Hypatia's question rather than Odelia's. "He's resting now and should do so until dinner. I've told Mr. Doolin that he'll have to bring in something for his dinner. Please thank Hilda for the breakfast tray."

"Of course, dear," Odelia crooned. "You know that our Hilda is ever ready to perform charitable acts. Poor man."

"You don't have anything else to tell us?" Magnolia asked, eyes narrowing. As usual, Mags wore a dark, nondescript shirtwaist dress, her long, steel-gray braid curving against one shoulder. On any day but Sunday, she might well be shod in rubber boots. Instead, in deference to the Sabbath, she wore penny loafers.

Kaylie knew that she was asking if Kaylie would come to their rescue by agreeing to provide nursing care for their unfortunate guest, but Kaylie was not yet prepared to commit to that. She could not make any promises until she had prayed the matter through and discussed it with her father. The aunts had to understand that.

"It wouldn't hurt if you checked in on him from time to time this evening," Kaylie said softly, answering Magnolia's question as deftly she was able.

"I'll be glad to look in on the poor boy," Odelia said brightly.

Hypatia, however, was not so sanguine. She even displayed a little annoyance. "Of course we'll look in on him, but that young man requires nursing care."

"He does," Kaylie admitted, then she took pity on them, adding, "I've promised an answer by tomorrow morning."

Hypatia dipped her chin. Slimmer than her sisters and still clad in the handsome gray silk suit that she'd worn to services that morning, her silver hair coiled into a smooth figure eight at the nape of her neck and pearls glowing softly at her throat, she might have been bestowing favors—or demerits—at court. Kaylie had to bite her tongue to keep from proclaiming that she would take on Stephen Gallow's care at once, but she knew too well what her father's reaction to that would be.

"I suppose we'll see you in the morning, then," Hypatia said primly.

"As soon as Dad sits down to his breakfast," Kaylie confirmed with a nod.

"Your father used to make his own breakfast," Magnolia pointed out with a sniff.

"Yes, I know." Her father used to do a lot of things that he seemed determined no longer to do. "Now I must get home." She rose and moved toward the door.

"Thank you for coming by, dear!" Odelia chirped. "Tell brother we'll have him to dinner soon, why don't you?"

"I'll do that," Kaylie replied, rushing through the foyer. "See you tomorrow."

She closed the door behind her with a sigh of relief before starting across the porch and down the steps to the boxy little red convertible that waited at the edge of the deeply graveled drive. She really needed some time alone. Her father had no doubt fed himself from the roast and vegetables that she'd left in the Crock-Pot that morning, and her own stomach was too tied in knots to allow her hunger to plague her. The sooner she took this matter to God, however, the sooner she would have her answer. And the sooner God's plan for them all, Stephen Gallow included, could come to fruition, for a plan He must have. The Almighty always did.

"Such a darling that girl is," Odelia said with a sigh. "She reminds me a good deal of you, Hypatia."

"Nonsense," Hypatia said, sipping from her teacup. "I would never have allowed Hubner to get out of hand as he has."

Well, that was true, Odelia had to concede. Hypatia never let anything or anyone get out of hand, while Odelia, conversely, seldom had things in hand. Like now. She'd only wanted to help, though. Perhaps she and Kaylie were more alike than she'd realized. Kaylie always sought to please everyone around her all the time. She had allowed Hub to take advantage of her to the point that she hardly had a life of her own anymore. Odelia bit her bright pink lip.

"Feeling sorry for himself, at his age," Magnolia grumbled about their brother. "We don't sit around feeling sorry for ourselves."

"Oh, but we have each other," Odelia pointed out.

"Our brother has four adult children, three granddaughters and two great-grandsons," Hypatia pointed out.

"And he's been blessed with love twice," Mags added.

"That's right!" Odelia said with a happy giggle. Trust her sisters to put everything into proper perspective. "Perhaps he'll even be blessed a third time!"

"At his age?" Mags snorted, recoiling.

"What has age got to do with it?" Odelia wanted to know. Surely Magnolia wasn't hinting that romantic love had forever passed them by. Why should that be?

"I hardly think," Hypatia interceded sternly, "that Hubner will find a third wife in time for Kaylie to decide she isn't needed by him so she can help us with our…guest."

Problem, she had been about to say. But not *their* problem. Oh, no, Stephen Gallow was more rightly Odelia's problem. Squelching a sigh, she put on a wobbly smile.

"I'm quite sure it will all work out for the best."

"God willing," Hypatia inserted. "Be that as it may, it was not well done of you, Odelia, obligating us to take in this… this…"

"Hockey player," Magnolia supplied, her tone leaving little doubt that she considered the man a ruffian of the worst sort. Last night's unhappy contretemps had only confirmed that opinion.

Odelia bowed her head in contrition. Hypatia was right about her obligating the sisters unfairly. But what was she supposed to have done? There she was, sitting in Brooks's waiting room, having made an appointment for her yearly physical, when suddenly she'd been swept into his office and told about this poor, injured man who hadn't a place in the world to go and hardly anyone to care for him. It had sounded so reasonable the way Brooks had explained it all, and when he'd asked it as a personal favor, well, what could she do but say yes? And the payment they'd offered!

Well, of course, the Chatams never accepted payment for kindness, but there was the new single parents' ministry at the Downtown Bible Church to consider. She'd thought that worthwhile project would welcome a hefty contribution. Still, the sisters had barely settled back into their normal routine after their nephew Reeves had moved from Chatam House, with his bride, Anna, and daughter, Gilli, before along came Mr. Gallow. If only he had not so quickly proven to be such a *presence* in the house.

"I'm sure God will work it all out for the best," Odelia offered meekly. "If Kaylie does decide to help us, even Hub will benefit, don't you think? He'll have to take up his life again, then. Yes?"

"You could be right," Hypatia said after a moment.

"I agree," Magnolia added reluctantly. "But just so you know—" she glared at Odelia "—whatever happens, I, for one, will *not* be emptying any bedpans."

Odelia felt the color drain from her face. Oh, dear. Surely it wouldn't come to that. No one could expect them to… Quickly, she set aside her teacup and held out her hands.

"Sisters," she said earnestly, "I feel the need to pray."

Chapter Three

Clasping her hands together, Kaylie bowed her head over the evening meal. "Father God, we thank You and praise You on this, Your Sabbath Day," she prayed. "You have restored Dad's health and given us lives of comfort and security. Bless Bayard and his family, Morgan and Chandler, the aunts and all our Chatam kin. Turn our minds ever to Your service, Lord, and let us not forget that we serve You only by serving others—which reminds me, Father, of that poor Mr. Gallow whom the aunts have taken in. Heal him, Lord, in such a way as to bring glory to Yourself, so that he is forever aware of Your love and power. Direct our paths, Father, and make Your will known to us, and finally, bless this food to the nourishment of our bodies. These things we pray in the name of Your Holy Son, Jesus the Christ. Amen."

"Amen," Hub Chatam echoed.

Dressed simply in black slacks and a white shirt, Hub unbuttoned and rolled back the cuffs of his sleeves before picking up his fork. His thinning hair, a mixture of light brown and ash-gray, seemed at odds with his bushy white eyebrows and dark brown eyes. Pushing up his bifocals with the tip of one finger, he trained those dark eyes on his daughter.

Kaylie had turned the remnants of his lunch into a hearty beef stew for their dinner, serving it with buttered bread and prepackaged salad. She kept her gaze carefully averted, applying herself to her meal. For several moments, silence reigned in the cozy, outdated kitchen, broken only by the clink of flatware. Kaylie could feel the comment coming, however, and finally it arrived.

"You waxed eloquent this evening, Kaylie."

She smiled. "Did I? Guess that's what comes of spending time praying."

"That's what you were doing this afternoon, sitting out in the backyard in the lawn chair? You were praying?"

Nodding, she scooped up a bite of stew. "Spring is a wonderful time to talk to God out of doors. I couldn't resist."

"Little warm for mid-April," her father muttered.

"Mm. We could be in for a hot summer."

"When have we not?"

Kaylie chuckled. "True."

Conversation lagged for a few minutes, and finally they got to the crux of the matter. "Who is this Mr. Gallow you mentioned? I assume he is the reason you dumped me after church and raced off to answer your aunts' beck and call."

Kaylie sighed mentally. Her father never used to be snide and self-centered. As a pastor, he had been one of the most caring, giving, selfless men she'd ever known, working long hours in the service of others. He had built Downtown Bible into a thriving, growing community of believers with vibrant worship, Scripturally sound doctrine and effective ministry. After choosing about a decade ago to allow a younger generation to lead the church into a new era, he had stepped aside as senior pastor, but neither the membership nor the new administration had been willing to truly let him go.

At their urging, he had assumed the position of Pastor of Congregational Care. The church's ministry to the home-bound and marginalized had expanded significantly under his tutelage. Part of the job had been organizing teams to check on, visit and minister to those sometimes invisible members, but Hubner Chatam had never been a mere administrator, and he'd often spent five, even six, days of every week in the field.

Then her mother, Kathryn, had died, and Hub never quite seemed to recover from her loss, perhaps because he had been widowed once before. The mother of Kaylie's two older brothers, Bayard and Morgan, had died of an accidental blow to the head when a hammer had fallen from a tall shelf. After losing his second wife, Hub had lost his zeal for ministry—and his zeal for life along with it. Chandler, her only full sibling, maintained that their father had grieved and resented his way into his heart attack. Kaylie only knew that he had become a very unhappy man, so she let go the remark about her "dumping" him.

"The aunts have taken him in as a favor to Brooks," she said, knowing that the doctor was one of Hub's favorite people. The good doctor had also lost a wife, to an inoperable brain tumor, and that seemed to have formed a bond between the two men.

Hub put down his fork thoughtfully. "Dr. Leland is not one to impose."

"No, he isn't."

"What's wrong with this Gallow?"

Kaylie sipped water from the tumbler beside her plate and said, "He was seriously injured in an accident."

"What sort of accident?"

Kaylie wrinkled her brow. "I don't think anyone ever said."

Hub clucked his tongue and shook his head, muttering, "Gallow, Gallow, unusual name. Don't believe I know any Gallows. Where is he from?"

"Actually," she answered with some surprise, "I believe he's originally from the Netherlands."

"The Netherlands! You don't say! Dutch then, is he?"

"You wouldn't know it to hear him speak," Kaylie said.

"What about his relatives? Surely you spoke with them."

Folding her hands in her lap, Kaylie shook her head. "Aren't any. At least, none near enough to help out."

"Ah. So your aunts, at the urging of Brooks Leland, have opened the family home to him," Hub deduced, "and now they find him more of a burden than they expected."

Kaylie nodded, "I'm afraid so."

"And because you're a nurse they expect you to deal with him."

"I do seem the logical choice," Kaylie pointed out.

Hubner waved a hand in agitation. "Do they not realize the level of your responsibilities?"

"I would say that the 'level of my responsibilities' is extremely light," Kaylie told him. "I've been thinking, in fact, that it might be time for me to go back to work at the hospital."

Her father sat back, clearly appalled. "But that would require shift work! You'd be gone all hours of the day and night."

Kaylie had considered that, and now she quite shamelessly used it. "Hm. Yes, I suppose that's true. Taking care of Mr. Gallow would be much less time-consuming. His injuries are serious, and his meds must be administered by a professional, but he's well enough to leave the hospital, at least. A couple hours in the morning, a couple hours in the afternoon and evening… I'd be home every night, free to get you your meals and your pills."

Hub considered, frowning at her, but eventually he accepted the obvious. Neither of them could, with a clear Christian conscience, say no. Hub grimaced.

"I blame my sisters for this. Once again, their 'project' means work for others."

"Dad!"

"You know it's true. Oh, I'm sure their hearts are in the right places, but never do their good works consist of labor only for them." He tossed up a gnarled hand. "Whatever they take on, it always requires teams of volunteers and committees of…committees! They're never satisfied until the whole of Buffalo Creek is involved. I suppose I should be thankful that we don't live any closer to Dallas. Imagine what causes they could get embroiled in there."

Kaylie bit back a smile, partly because he was right. Somewhat. The aunts did tend to take on huge schemes like raising funds for the Buffalo Creek Bible College and the local free clinic. Lately their pet project was one that Hub had once championed himself, ministries and services aimed at single-parent households. The aunts were preparing, as Hypatia put it, to take that initiative to a "whole new level."

"Maybe Mr. Gallow is more than they can manage on their own," she said, "but this time it's just me involved, and I expect to be paid for my expertise."

"Oh, yes, throw money at the problem," Hub said, "as if the Chatam well will never run dry. Your brother Bayard has warned them time and again."

A staunchly conservative banker, Bayard constantly harped on the idea that the aunts, now approaching their mid-seventies, *could* outlive their inheritance, as if they lived profligately. The aunties and most of the rest of the family, including Hub until recently, pretty much just tuned him out.

"You misunderstand. The aunts aren't paying me, Dad. Mr. Gallow is."

"Oh. Well, I suppose that if he's getting free room and board, he can afford to pay for private nursing care."

Kaylie supposed that he could pay for a lot more than that, but she didn't say so. Why open the door for questions that she would rather not have to answer? Like where Stephen

Gallow's money came from, for instance. Having run out of reasons for complaint, at the moment, Hubner went back to his meal, and Kaylie turned her silent thoughts to how best to serve her new patient.

"Good morning."

Stephen opened his eyes to the now familiar sound of the gentle, slightly husky but decidedly feminine voice. He'd been awake for some time, actually, the throbbing in his bones keeping him still, while he worried about his situation with the team.

The playoffs were now officially under way, and though he had been the goalie to get the team there for the first time in their short history, he had been out of the pipes for nearly two weeks now, with weeks more to go before he could even think about starting rehab. He wasn't going to see ice time again this season, so should the team actually win the Stanley Cup—a long shot but feasible—his part in the triumph could well be forgotten. Of course, it was entirely possible that, given the good conduct clause in his contract, the team might cut or trade him regardless of what happened in the playoffs, especially if his backup, Kapimsky, proved able to get the job done.

Stephen had expected Aaron, bleary from a night spent in a strange bed, to be the first person he saw this morning, and though he would never admit it, Stephen dearly wanted his agent's reassurance. Instead, he would have to settle for the ministrations of the new nurse. At least he hoped that she had decided to take the position. He turned his head slightly to find Kaylie Chatam regarding him serenely from the open doorway.

He smiled, for two reasons. One, the petite nurse's soft red hair hung down her back in a thick, straight tail of pure silk at least as long as his forearm. Secondly, she was dressed for work in shapeless pink scrubs with surfing penguins printed on them.

"In the Netherlands," he told her, "they say '*Goedemorgen.*'"

"Gude morgan, then."

He tried not to correct her pronunciation, covering his amusement by saying, "Penguins?"

She plucked at the fabric of her loose top, looking down at a penguin tumbling through a cresting wave. "Best I could do. No skates, but at least they're creatures that are comfortable on the ice."

He laughed. And regretted it. Squeezing his eyes shut against the sharpened pain, he hissed until it subsided to a more bearable level. When he opened his eyes again, Kaylie Chatam was standing over him, pill bottle in hand.

"Mr. Doolin's gone down to ask for your breakfast tray. Let's get these into you so you'll be up to eating when it's ready. All right?"

"Fine," he grumbled. "But then I need to get to the bathroom."

She dropped the pill bottle into one of the cavernous pockets on the front of her smock and slid her small but surprisingly strong hands beneath his arms, helping him into a sitting position on the side of the bed. He tried to bite back the groan that accompanied the action, but the pain was breathtaking. It eased as soon as he was still again. She quickly gave him the pills. After swallowing a pair of them, he was ready to go forward. He shoved up onto his good leg, jaw clamped.

Moving effortlessly into a supportive posture, Kaylie slid her arm up over his back to his shoulder, her own shoulder tucked neatly beneath his arm. Hopping and hobbling, he inched toward the bathroom door. Small bathrooms, he mused a few minutes later, had their good points, as the close confines allowed him to manage for himself. Afterward, the little nurse made a very welcome suggestion.

"Maybe you should eat your breakfast in the sitting room."

Stephen looked into the sitting room and smiled. Comfortable as it was, the bed had already begun to feel like a prison to him.

"If it's any inducement," she went on in a teasing voice, "there's a large cup of coffee in there."

Stephen eagerly slung his arm around her shoulders. "Lead me to it."

Chuckling, she eased him forward. By the time they reached the near end of the sofa, some three or four yards, his head swam. Bracing her feet wide apart and gripping his one good arm, she helped him lower into a sitting position in the corner of the comfortable couch before fetching a small, brocade footstool for his injured leg.

"How's that?"

He waited until the pain subsided enough that he could get his breath. "Guess I'll live. What about that coffee?"

While she went to the small writing desk standing against one wall and retrieved a tall, disposable cup with a cardboard sleeve, Stephen looked around him. Oddly elegant paintings that featured game birds, dogs and tools of the hunt from a bygone era covered the walls of the room. In contrast to the antique artwork, he noted, with relieved satisfaction, a flat-screen television hung over the mantel. The old girls didn't have their heads entirely buried in the past, then. The screen was nowhere near as large as the one in his media room back at the house in Fort Worth, but it would do for watching the playoff games.

Stephen took the coffee container from Kaylie with his good right hand, turning it with the aid of the fingertips of his left to get the drinking slot in the plastic top adequately positioned. Taking a careful sip, he sighed with satisfaction.

"I have cream, if you'd like," she said, reaching into her pocket once more and drawing out the tiny containers.

"Black is fine."

Nodding, she parked her hands at her slender hips and glanced around before snapping her fingers and hurrying back into the bedroom. "Hang on."

Like I'm going anywhere, he thought wryly. She returned an instant later with one of the bed pillows and a bath towel.

"We'll have to keep using this as a lap tray until I find one," she explained, placing the pillow across his lap. She covered both it and his chest with the towel.

He slugged back more of the coffee. It was still hot but thoroughly drinkable, and he moaned in delight as the silky brew flowed down his throat.

"Wonderful," he said, using his thumb to tidy the corners of his lips. "This is the best cup of coffee I've had in weeks. Thank you."

"My pleasure," she said, smiling down at him, and oddly enough, he thought that it just might be. She actually seemed pleased that he enjoyed the coffee. Something about that struck him as… Well, it just struck him.

He had little time to puzzle over the matter as Aaron carried his breakfast tray into the room just then. Despite being rumpled and unshaven, Aaron whistled cheerily as he crossed the floor.

"It's a good thing I'm a married man again," he said at his jocular best, "or else I'd have to take that Hilda away from poor old Chester. That woman can cook! Mmm-mmm."

At the word *again,* Stephen saw Kaylie's eyebrows rise ever so slightly. Silently amused, he glanced innocently at Aaron as Kaylie moved aside so he could deposit the tray on the pillow across Stephen's lap.

Belgian waffles, still steaming from the iron, sliced strawberries, maple syrup, ham and—Stephen couldn't believe his eyes—*gele room.* Kaylie touched the rim of the fluted cup of thick, sweet, golden cream with the tip of one finger.

"Clotted cream, a bit of England right here in the very heart of Texas." Her dark eyes twinkled merrily. "My aunts are devoted to all things English."

Stephen had no idea why that might be, but he didn't care. Setting aside the coffee, he picked up his fork with his left fingers and his knife with his right. It was awkward, and he got cream on the edge of his jacket sling, but he managed to cut up the waffle. Nurse Kaylie watched intently, but she did not offer to cut up his breakfast for him. He liked her for that.

Aaron took his suit jacket and tie from the desk chair and began putting them on, chatting happily. "Our darling nurse has given me a shopping list, Steve-o. I'll just make a quick run into the picturesque town of Buffalo Creek, and then it's home to the little bride." He clapped a hand on Stephen's shoulder. "I leave you in capable, if dainty, hands." He bowed over one of those dainty hands like some sort of old gallant, saying grandly, "I'd kiss your pretty little pink toes, darlin', if I wasn't married."

"Again," Kaylie chirped, looking a bit startled with herself, as well as amused.

"Hey," Aaron quipped good-naturedly, "third time's the charm, right?"

He waved and strode happily from the room. Kaylie pressed a hand to her chest and looked at Stephen.

"Has he really been married three times?"

Stephen nodded, going to work on his ham. "Never knew the first one, but anyone could have told him that was a no-go. She was, er, an exotic dancer. The, um, second wife," he went on, "used him as a stepping stone to the bigger things."

"Bigger things?"

Putting down his knife, Stephen took up his fork with his right hand, though he still had some difficulty eating that way. "Aaron's second wife left him for a hockey player," he told Kaylie bluntly, "after Aaron negotiated a six-million-dollar contract for the guy." He gave her the name, but since it obviously meant nothing to her, he added, "The creep's a starting center on the East Coast now."

"Ah."

"I think Aaron maybe got it right this time," Stephen went on. "I think Dora loves him. She sure acts like it. Behaves as if he's the cleverest, wittiest thing she's ever met." He shook his head.

Nurse Chatam slid her small hands into her big pockets. "He is kind of funny."

Stephen chuckled and forked up another bite. "He is, really, especially when you get to know him. Fact is, Aaron's a good guy."

"But you give him a hard time anyway," the little nurse remarked softly.

Stephen stilled. He did. He really did give Aaron a hard time. He wondered why. But then he knew. He gave Aaron a hard time because Aaron did not give him one when he clearly deserved it. Suddenly chilled, tired and irritated, Stephen dropped his fork and tugged at the neck of his T-shirt, the armhole of which had been slit to accommodate the cast on his left arm before the jacket sling went on. The back of the sofa had tugged it askew, and the stupid thing was choking him.

Seeing the problem, the little nurse leaned close and reached behind him to pull up the fabric of his shirt, loosening the pressure on his throat. She smelled clean and sweet, like the air after a spring rain, and Stephen felt a sudden longing. In some ways, that longing made him think of his boyhood and his mother, but the feeling was in no way childlike. He suddenly wondered just what the next several weeks might hold. Who was this petite, Bible-quoting lovely, anyway, and why did she make him feel clumsy and ignorant?

Waiting until she straightened, he turned a bland face up

at her and asked, "What should I call you? Nurse seems a bit impersonal."

"Kaylie will do."

"All right, Kaylie. And I'm Stephen. Or Steve, if you prefer."

"But not Stevie," she said, a quirk at one corner of her lips.

"Not Stevie," he confirmed. Stevie had been a boy whose parents had tugged him this way and that between them, an innocent who had ceased to exist decades ago, mourned by no one, not even him, though he had been that boy. "So, Kaylie," he said, changing the subject, "tell me something about yourself."

"Not much to tell. What do you want to know?"

He really wanted to know if she was married or involved with anyone, but he had more game than to ask outright. "Well," he said, pondering his options, "so, um, where do you live exactly? I know you don't live here."

She shook her head. "No. No, I don't live here. I live with my father, about three miles across town."

With her father? Interesting. Odd, but interesting. What woman her age lived with her father? That brought up another question.

"And, uh, how old are you?"

"Twenty-four."

That was about what he'd figured, despite the air of inexperience about her.

She leaned forward, her hands clasped behind her back, to ask, "And you?"

"Twenty-eight." Felt more like eighty-two of late. He put on a smile and said, "I take it you're not married. I mean, since you live with your father."

"Uh, no, not married."

"Engaged?"

"No."

"Dating?"

She blinked at him, tilting her head. "Forgive me, but I don't see how that is relevant."

Feeling thwarted and a tad irritated, he waved a hand. "Sorry. Just making conversation. I can't help being a little curious, though, since you live with your father still."

"Not *still*," she said pointedly. "Again." He waited for her to go on, and after a slight pause, she did. "My father is seventy-six years old and suffered a heart attack a few months ago. I moved in to take care of him."

"What about your mother?" Stephen asked.

"Deceased." The way she said it told him that the death had been fairly recent.

"Sorry to hear that."

Lifting her head, she beamed a soft smile and said, "Thank you."

That smile took his breath away, rocked him right down to the marrow of his bones. The sincerity, not to mention the beauty, of it was downright shocking. No one in his world was that open and genuine.

After a moment of awkward silence, she glanced around the room, before blurting, "My brothers expected it of me."

Knocked back into the conversation, Stephen cleared his throat and marshaled his mental processes. "They, ah, expected you to take care of your father, you mean?"

She nodded. "They're all older, and I'm the only girl, and a nurse, too."

"I see. What if you hadn't wanted to take care of him, though?"

"I did!" she exclaimed quickly.

"Did?"

"Do!" she corrected. "I do want to take care of him."

"But?" he pressed, certain that some caveat existed.

She bit her lip then fluttered her hands. "You have to understand that he's been widowed twice over the years, and since he left the church, he's been at loose ends."

"Left the church?"

"Retired, I should have said. Retired from the church."

Carefully, to prevent any misunderstanding, Stephen asked, "He worked for the church?"

"He's a minister," she said, confirming Stephen's worst fears. "Or was a minister. *Is* a minister," she finally decided with a sigh. "He just isn't active in ministry right now."

Stephen's mind reeled. So she was not just a Christian, she was the daughter of a Christian minister! "With three brothers, no less." He hadn't realized that he'd muttered that last aloud until she addressed the comment.

"Yes, well, two are half brothers, to be precise, and a good deal older. Bayard's fifty-five, and Morgan's forty-two."

"Fifty-five!" Stephen echoed, shocked. "My mother's only fifty-three."

"My mom would be fifty-eight. She died two years ago."

"So your dad was nearly twenty years older than her."

"Yes. It just didn't seem that way until she got sick. He aged a dozen years during the weeks of her illness, and he hasn't been the same since."

"My father hasn't been the same since my parents' divorce," Stephen said, to his own surprise. Realizing how personal the conversation had become, he quickly changed directions. "What was it you sent Aaron after?"

She ticked off a list of items. "Hand sanitizer, antibacterial soap, lip balm, sterile gloves, syringes… The doctor called in a new prescription, by the way, injections that should help you control your pain better."

Stephen let that go without comment, but he was desperately tired of all these drugs. He felt as if he was sleeping—

and dreaming—his life away. The dreams, unfortunately, were not pleasant ones. Kaylie, he noticed, tapped her chin, staring at him as if trying to read his mind.

"I wonder if I should have asked for leverage straps?"

"Leverage straps?" Stephen parroted. "Whatever for?"

"To get you up and down more easily," she explained. "I'm not very big, you know, and you're—"

"Six foot four," he supplied, "and over two hundred pounds."

"Exactly."

"Still," Stephen pointed out, "we've managed pretty well so far, and I'm only going to get better, you know."

"Hmm, I suppose." She continued tapping her chin, the tip of her finger fitting nicely into the tiny cleft there. More a dimple, really, Stephen had begun to think it a charming feature. "Maybe I should've asked for a lap tray, too," she murmured, staring down at the remnants of his breakfast.

"Now that I'll go with," Stephen said. "Why don't I call Aaron and add that to the list? No, wait. I don't have a cell phone any longer." His had been destroyed in the accident, along with his car and half his house.

"You can use mine," she said, producing a small flip phone from those seemingly bottomless pockets.

"Better yet," Stephen said, "let's text him. Then he has it in writing."

"Oh," she replied casually, "my phone doesn't text."

Stephen's jaw dropped. "You're kidding." Stunned, he stared up at her. "You're not kidding!" Who, in this day and age, didn't have text?

Kaylie, of the dark, bottomless eyes and heavy, light red hair, tilted her head. "Is that a problem?"

"Yeah, it could be. Like, what if I need you in the middle of the night or something?" He ignored for now the fact that he didn't have a cell phone himself. "Do you want me waking up the entire the household by shouting or even by ringing you? Or would you rather I sent you a nice quiet text message?"

"Oh, I won't be staying the night here," Kaylie told him calmly.

"Won't be staying—" Stephen broke off, momentarily dumbstruck. "But I thought you were taking the job!"

"I am. I just won't be here at night—or whenever you're sleeping."

"B-but what if something happens?"

"Such as?"

Such as nightmares, he thought, dreams that tormented him until he woke writhing and screaming, memories about which he could not bring himself to speak. He hated the weakness and guilt that allowed the horrific dreams to flourish, and the second accident seemed to have brought back the memories of the first one in all its horrific detail, details he'd give almost anything to forget.

"I don't know!" he snapped in answer to her question. "You tell me. You're the nurse."

She patted his shoulder consolingly. "Now don't worry. The aunts will look in on you, and there's always the staff. Hilda, Chester and Carol have been taking care of Chatam House and its occupants for over twenty years, you know. They do, however, have Sundays and Wednesdays off."

"You mean the cook, and that old bald guy I met when I first got here?" Stephen protested.

"Chester's not old," Kaylie argued with a smile. "Why, he's just barely sixty!"

"But what if I fall out of bed or trip on my way to the bathroom?"

Kaylie Chatam folded her arms, looking down at him with the patience and authority that a particularly wise adult might reserve for an unreasonable child. "You'll be fine as long as you don't try to get up and about on your own too soon. I'll make sure you're properly settled in before I leave, and I will, after all, be just a phone call away."

A phone call and three miles, he wanted to snarl. Well, if that's the way she wanted to play it, he would make doubly sure of her availability. He held out his hand, instructing, "Give me the cell phone."

Frowning, she produced the phone and dropped it into his palm. Stephen flipped it open and punched in the numbers with his thumb before hitting the send button and lifting the tiny phone to his ear. After several rings, Aaron answered. Stephen interrupted his effusive greeting and got right down to business.

"You're going to have to make another stop or two. Seems Kaylie would like to add a lap tray to her shopping list, so I don't have to eat off the bed pillows. Then I need you to do something for me. I want two cell phones with texting, Internet access, global positioning and anything else you can think of. One for me, one for our Nurse Chatam, who will not, as it turns out, be working full-time."

"Even full-time is not around-the-clock," she pointed out, parking her hands at her slender waist.

"For the money we're paying you, it ought to be!" Stephen snapped. Then he barked into the phone, "Just do it, Aaron," and hung up.

He passed the phone back to her, glowering. He didn't know why he was so upset, really. Just last night, he'd argued that Aaron didn't have to stay, and truth be told, the fewer people who knew about his nightmares, the better. Yet, he found that he'd been looking forward to having Kaylie Chatam around. She seemed to bring a certain serenity with her, an assurance that, temporarily at least, banished his worries and made him believe that he could put yet another stupid, ugly episode behind him.

But who was he kidding? Some things could never be gotten over. Some decisions, some disasters, could not be left in the past. They could only be lived with, one torturous day at a time.

So be it, he decided angrily.

His past had left him with enough pain to go around, and he was suddenly in the mood to share.

Chapter Four

Stephen Gallow, Kaylie decided, was as much child as adult. Honestly, the way he pouted! Then again, she should be used to it by now, for his behavior really was not much different from her father's. Men! What was it that made them such impossible patients? Either they were too macho to give in to disease or, once overwhelmed by it, they wallowed in black despair and petulant behavior.

She thought of her mother and how patiently and cheerfully that dear woman had endured her own swift decline: dizziness so acute that she couldn't stand without retching, vision so blurry that she could neither read nor watch television, pain so intense that there were whole days she could not lift her head from her pillow. At the end, she could not swallow even her own saliva, but she had smiled with gratitude every time someone had wiped her mouth for her. When relief had finally come, she had passed into the next life with the most peaceful expression imaginable. And Hubner Chatam had been angry ever since.

Why, Kaylie wondered, was Stephen Gallow angry? For angry he definitely was, so much so that she probably ought to tell him to keep his job or find someone else more to his liking. But she didn't. Instead, she remained mute, for what if she offered him her resignation and he took her up on it? After all, if taking the job was God's will for her, then she had no business resigning it.

If that explanation did not entirely satisfy, she chose not to search for another.

Stephen expressed a sudden weariness, so she got him to his feet and helped him hobble back to the bed, his rapidly failing strength burdening both of them. Doolin came in just as they reached the bed, his arms laden with bags.

"Are you sure we didn't forget something?" he quipped, dumping the bags on the chest at the foot of the bed. "I could've bought a nice gurney while I was out or a coffee plantation in Brazil. Hospital, anyone? I hear there's a good one in Galveston, right on the beach. Palm trees, sun and sand."

"Hurricanes," Stephen growled, easing down onto the edge of the bed.

"Always looking on the bright side," Aaron joked, digging into the bags. "Got those phones," he said to his client, "and just in the nick of time. You'll never guess who called. Okay, you will, because she's been calling ever since you drove your car through your house."

Kaylie gasped. "Is that what happened?" She looked at Stephen. "You drove your car through your house? But how is that possible?"

They both studiously ignored her questions. Instead, Stephen glared at Aaron. "You did *not* give her my new number. Tell me you did not give her my new number."

"I didn't give her your new number," Aaron said dryly, huffing slightly as if Stephen had questioned his loyalty. "That way she can keep calling me and pleading to speak to you."

Stephen looked away. "Tell her I'll talk to her when I'm better."

"I've been telling her that. She says if she doesn't speak to you soon, she's coming over here."

Stephen seemed to dismiss that out of hand. "She doesn't know where I am."

"She knows where I am," Aaron pointed out. "She knows where the arena is and the team offices."

Stephen's head jerked around, an appalled look on his face, but then he sighed. "I can't deal with this now, Aaron. Find a way to put her off. Now, give me the phones."

Aaron threw up his hands and went back to pawing through the bags. "I'm just saying…"

Confused and curious, Kaylie helped Stephen into a prone position.

"Get me the other pillow, will you?" he mumbled, his gaze averted. "I've spent enough time flat on my back."

"All right."

She went to do as requested, aware of Stephen and Aaron speaking quietly together in the next room. She returned with the second pillow and, after making Stephen comfortable in a semi-reclining position, she distributed the goods about the room, placing each item where it would be most handy. Meanwhile, Aaron and Stephen discussed the phones and their functions. Eventually, they called her over, and Aaron explained what amounted to a miniature handheld computer with a touch screen, camera, microphone and speaker. The thing was amazing and must have cost a fortune. She turned over the sleek contraption in her hand and looked to Stephen.

"This really isn't necessary, you know."

"I think it is," he said dismissively, failing to meet her gaze.

Aaron jumped in, using his "good buddy" voice. "I've programmed in Steve's new number, mine and the doc's. The roll-up keyboard works like this." He demonstrated, adding,

"Makes it easier if you're not used to phone-pad texting. This way you just type."

"Okay," Kaylie said, pocketing the sleek new gadget. "If you say so."

"One thing," Stephen insisted, deigning to look at her. "I want your word that you'll keep that with you at all times. Understood?"

Kaylie just barely refrained from rolling her eyes. "I'll keep it with me at all times. And when you don't need my assistance anymore, I'll return it."

Stephen bobbed his head in a curt nod. Aaron split an uncertain look between the two of them and clapped his hands together with forced joviality. "Okeydoke. I am off to see the little woman." He walked backward toward the door. "Either of you need anything, you give me a shout." He paused in the doorway long enough to point a finger at Stephen and say, "I'll see you in a day or two, kid. You behave yourself and let nurse darlin' take care of you. Understand?" He winked at Kaylie and blew her a noisy kiss, exclaiming, "Angel of mercy!" With that, he turned and hurried from sight.

Stephen put his head back and closed his eyes, dismissing her as effectively as if he'd turned his back on her. Unfortunately for him, she'd had a good deal of recent experience in dealing with hardheaded men. Leaning a shoulder against the bedpost at the foot of the bed, she folded her arms and regarded him thoughtfully. Kaylie very much wanted to ask Stephen about the "she" whose phone call to Aaron Doolin had so obviously upset him earlier, but she had no plausible professional reason for doing so. She didn't see anything to be gained by taking him to task for his attitude, but the accident, on the other hand, seemed well within her purview, her personal curiosity aside.

"It might help me to know about your accident," she said after a long moment of silence.

He opened an eye and peered down his nose at her. Closing that eye again, he settled more comfortably. She assumed that would be the end of it, but just as she dropped her arms and started to straighten away from the bedpost, he spoke.

"I accidentally drove my car through the garage wall and into my house. What else do you want to know?"

Horrified, she shook her head, grasping the bedpost with both hands. "How on earth did such a thing happen?"

Sighing richly, he opened both eyes and stared up at the ceiling. "Some friends had driven my car and left it parked outside with the top down and a storm threatening." Kaylie winced. "Worried that the storm would ruin the interior, I rushed out to move the car into the garage, but when I should have hit the brake, I accidentally hit the gas pedal."

"Oh, my, and in a convertible, no less."

"A very expensive convertible with a powerful engine. Powerful enough to propel me through two walls and right into a free-standing fireplace."

"Goodness!"

"Nothing good about it," he said sourly. "Not only was the car ruined, the house all but came down."

"No wonder your injuries are so serious!"

He lifted a hand to his head, as if holding down the top of it. "Nothing I don't deserve for being so incredibly stupid. *Idiotic dwass,*" he muttered.

She didn't need to know Dutch to understand the gist of that. Her heart went out to him. He might be a spoiled sports figure, but he was also a seriously injured man whose pride had obviously been as battered as his body.

Her father had his faith and his family to help him overcome his loss and his health issues, but what or who did Stephen Gallow have? Only himself and his sports agent, as far as she could see.

Was that why God had brought him here to Chatam House? Of course it must be. She'd already considered the possibility that Stephen Gallow's sudden presence in her family's life had to do with a loving God's plan for her father, but God continually reached out to all of His creation. She must not forget that fact. It was as if God's love for Stephen Gallow imbued her in that moment. Instinctively, she reached out a hand to him.

That hand fell upon the covers blanketing his foot, his huge foot. That foot would make two of hers, and yet, she sensed that deep inside he was as lost and troubled as any little boy alone in the world. He might be a gladiator on the ice, but here and now he was a wounded patient in need of a kind, caring hand.

"Can I get you anything?"

He shook his head.

"Are you in pain?"

"No more than usual." He flattened his mouth then said, "Not as much as earlier."

Accepting that she could do nothing more for him at the moment, she nodded and moved toward the door, saying, "I'll just take your breakfast tray down, then." Pausing, she looked back at him. "I could bring you a book. The aunties have quite a library, you know."

He lifted his eyebrows at that, but then he shrugged. Kaylie smiled and went out. She was halfway down the stairs, having left the tray in the dumbwaiter, when the new phone in her pocket dinged and vibrated. Surprised, she dug it out and peered at the screen.

It read, "Sports. Thrillers. Sci-fi. Westerns."

She understood that he was telling her what sorts of books he preferred, most likely in the order that he preferred them. Awkwardly, she typed out a return message, pecking at the tiny keyboard with the tip of her forefinger. "See what I can find."

She watched as the message went on its way, then she went on hers, shaking her head. How odd that Stephen seemed to find it easier to reveal his tastes in a text message rather than in person. That seemed to say something important about him, something sad.

As Kaylie had told Stephen, Hilda Worth and her husband, Chester, along with Hilda's sister Carol Petty, had been taking care of Kaylie's aunts and Chatam House for decades. The aunts considered them family, and since they lived in what had been the carriage house, they were ever-present fixtures about the estate, as much a part of it as the magnolia tree on the west lawn, the rose arbor on the east and the priceless antiques that comprised the majority of the furnishings. None of the family would treat the staff with less consideration than they would allow each other, which was why Kaylie went straight to the kitchen to clean up after her patient.

That was exactly where Aaron Doolin found her, up to her elbows in the enameled, cast-iron sink. She rinsed the last dish and set it in the folding wooden dish drainer next to the sink before drying her hands on a towel and turning to face him.

"I thought you left."

"Yeah, I thought I had, too, then I remembered to do what I'm paid to do." He waved a sheaf of papers at her.

"What are those?"

Doolin trained his practiced smile on her. "We never discussed salary and what all." It was the "what all" that made her narrow her eyes. Aaron rubbed hands together. "How does a thousand dollars a day sound?"

She laughed, thinking it was a joke. "Ridiculous."

He grimaced. "Okay, eleven hundred."

Oh, now, this was absurd. No wonder Stephen had expected around-the-clock availability. She parked her hands at her waist. "You can't be serious. What were you paying the last person?"

"Nine hundred," Aaron said, poking a finger at her. "What? You think we're trying to go on the cheap now, pay you less than the last guy? I can show you the canceled check, if you want."

It took several seconds for her to conclude that he meant it, and when she did, she could only shake her head. "Wow, did he ever see you coming. You can hire a private nurse at half the cost from any agency in the Metroplex area."

Aaron's salt-and-pepper brows shot up, but then he rubbed his chin, watching her as if she was some alien life form. "Did I forget to mention the nondisclosure contract? You can't talk about any of this, you know. Nada, nothing. Not a thing that has to do with Steve or his care."

"All medical personnel are forbidden by law to discuss their patients. Didn't they explain that to you at the hospital?"

Aaron looked perplexed. "Well, yeah, but the other guy said that only applied there."

"The 'other guy' was unscrupulous, then," she told him.

Doolin shrugged and declared, "Who knew! He came to me, said we'd need someone discreet. I'm no health professional. How was I supposed to figure out this stuff?"

Frowning, Kaylie folded her arms. "I'll be glad to give you an address where you can report him, if you like. I'm sure the hospital would be eager to know that one of their employees is soliciting private jobs, too."

Aaron cleared his throat and said, "Ah, maybe the less said there, the better. I mean, we're the ones trying to keep a low profile, right? So, um, what would you consider a fair daily fee?"

She told him, and he seemed dumbfounded for a moment. "Really?" he asked weakly.

"Really. Just don't expect more than eight hours a day

from me. As I've already explained to Stephen, I won't be spending nights here."

Doolin frowned warily. "Are you sure he'll be okay?"

"As long as he behaves sensibly."

"Good luck with that."

"Look, I'm not a babysitter. I'm a nurse." He opened his mouth to argue the point, but she cut him off. "All right, all right. That'll work itself out. Let's concentrate on one issue at a time. How about we do it this way? How about you pay me by the hour, then if the job requires more time than I think it will, we're all happy."

Doolin nodded. "Yeah, yeah, we'll keep track by phone. You send a text when you arrive and when you leave. I'll verify it with Stevie and write the check. What hourly rate were you thinking of?"

She told him, and the deal was at last struck. Evidently pleased with himself, Aaron beamed then scowled very sternly. "But you still have to sign the nondisclosure agreement. That's just how we roll on this."

Kaylie fought a smile. She could almost see him trying to negotiate a multimillion-dollar contract, all steely-eyed and tough one minute, happy as a puppy with a new ball the next. The man was less agent than actor. She quite liked him, and she liked Stephen Gallow for employing him.

"Whatever you say."

He went back to beaming, and she went back to trying to keep a straight face.

"Great! Don't mean to pressure you, but I have to protect my boy," Aaron prattled, clearly relishing the act. "He's got enough problems with the team as it is. We can't have anyone blabbing to the press."

"I don't blab to the press or anyone else, Mr. Doolin."

"Aaron," he corrected. "A woman of few words. I knew I liked you." He plopped the papers down on the enormous butcher-block work island in the center of the homey, brick-and-plaster room and produced an ink pen. "Now, if I can just get your John Henry…"

She dutifully signed the documents, which Aaron witnessed and dated. Stowing the ink pen with one hand, he gathered up the papers with the other, kissed them and stuffed them into a pocket of his coat. "Now I can get home to the missus."

"I, uh, just have one question for you," Kaylie said quickly, surprised at herself, though not for the first time that day.

"Sure. What's that?"

"What sort of problems does Stephen have with his team exactly?"

Aaron clapped a hand to the nape of his neck uneasily. "Why do you ask?"

The answer came to her only as it was falling out of her mouth. "So I can pray for him. An informed prayer is often more powerful than a vague one."

"Huh. I wondered just how that worked," Aaron said. "I mean, isn't God supposed to know everything already?"

"Absolutely, He does. Prayer is not for His sake. It's not as if we have to remind Him about what's going on in this world," she explained. "Prayer is for us. It's a tool for our benefit."

Aaron Doolin nodded his head, his lips curling up at one corner. "Okay, I can get behind that. So, lay it on the Big Guy, if you want. Most specifically, you can ask Him not to let the team cut or trade our boy. Not that I think they will for sure. It's just that there's this good-conduct clause in his contract, see, and, well, if they wanted to be sticklers about it…" He sighed, braced himself with a hand placed flat atop the work island and crossed his feet at the ankles. "It's like this, see.

About five years ago, when he first came into the league, there was this drunk-driving accident."

"Oh, dear," Kaylie said, dismayed. She almost wished she hadn't asked.

"Hey, Stevie was young and celebrating the fact that he'd finally made the big league. Anyway, he learned his lesson, a stiff one. Truly. Only the club insisted on the clause, and technically…"

"He was drunk when he drove his car through his house," she surmised softly.

"Technically," Aaron repeated with some force. "I mean, he was drinking, but he had a couple of buddies drive him home that night, which was the responsible thing to do. Right? If they hadn't left the car out with the top down and a storm hadn't blown up all of sudden it wouldn't have happened." Aaron spread his hands. "Steve was just parking the car in the garage, not driving. Not *really* driving."

Kaylie sighed. If her father ever got wind of this… She didn't even want to think about it. One of his chief complaints about her brother Chandler's chosen occupation was the abundance of alcohol surrounding the sport of rodeo. Still, she didn't want to have to defend Stephen Gallow to her father or even to discuss him at all if she could help it. She didn't want to have to choose between her father's approval and taking care of Stephen—mostly because she didn't know, at this point, which she would, should, choose.

She managed a smile for Aaron. "I understand."

"Hey, it's like I keep telling Stevie. As long as the press doesn't make a big deal of this, it'll blow over. In the meantime, I'll be there reminding management just who it was that got the team to the playoffs in the first place." He smoothed a hand down the front of his shirt, apparently forgetting that he wasn't wearing a tie, and added, "Little insurance wouldn't hurt, though. I mean, he could use somebody up there looking out for him, you know?"

She knew. Oh, yes, she knew. But she doubted that Stephen did.

"Thank you for confiding in me, Aaron."

"Aw, you're part of the team now, right? The Gallow team."

Kaylie let her smile speak for her. Flipping her a wave, Aaron sauntered away. Kaylie's smile faded to a frown of concern as he disappeared from sight.

The Gallow team. What neither Stephen nor Aaron seemed to understand was that it was much more important that they were all on God's team.

She heard a ding and felt a vibration. Rolling her eyes, she dug into her pocket for the new phone. This time the message read, "Where r u?"

Shaking her head, she typed a simple reply. "Kitchen. You ok?"

"Bored," read the message he sent back. "Hurry."

Electing to simply drop the phone into her pocket, she went to find a few books that might, hopefully, appeal to him. Technically, entertaining him was not her job, but representing Christ to him certainly was. She just hoped that she didn't regret letting him foist this phone on her.

Being in constant contact with Stephen Gallow was bound to turn her world upside down.

The stack of books stood almost a foot tall. Some hardbacks, some paperbacks, Kaylie had chosen them with as much care as her patient's incessant texting had allowed. Using his one good hand, Stephen went through the offerings skeptically. They included a baseball biography, a mystery, a couple of lawyer/suspense novels—he pointedly yawned at those—a nonfiction account of the historical exploits of a fellow named Joseph Walker and four books from a fiction series about the Second Coming of Christ.

"Those ought to keep you busy," Kaylie said in a satisfied tone.

"Or put me in a coma," Stephen grumbled, dumping the last book on top of what was now a jumble on the bedside table. As soon as she'd entered the room, he'd announced that he'd already checked the hockey news via the Internet on his new phone and scoped out some interesting downloads. Apparently, several games were being installed on the amazing little contraption as they conversed. He checked the progress of the installation and sighed.

"Oh, come on," she cajoled, waving a hand at the heap of books, "something there has to interest you."

He glanced once more at the bedside table before determinedly turning his head away. "I'm too tired to read right now."

"Then sleep for an hour or two," she suggested lightly.

His pale gray eyes instantly turned to ice. "Why? So you can disappear on me?"

Kaylie ignored that, making every effort to retain her patience. The man, after all, was in pain. As opposed to just being a pain. Glancing pointedly at her utilitarian wristwatch, she noted the time.

"I'll leave a few minutes before eleven to make Dad his lunch. Be back here just after noon to help with yours. You might want to clean up after that. Then I thought we might wrap your ribs, give you a little more stabilization in your torso so you can move more easily. The jacket sling helps, but it's not the best thing for your ribs." Aware of his deepening glower, she forged on. "By that time, you'll probably be needing another rest. I have some errands to run later this afternoon, but I'll return in time to give you dinner and meds. Can I bring you anything? Maybe some puzzles or a—"

He rolled his eyes, but before either could say more on the subject, they were interrupted.

"Yoo-hoo!"

Recognizing the voice, Kaylie turned toward the door. "Aunt Odelia?"

Footsteps clattered across the sitting room, then Odelia's stark white head, topped with a big floppy yellow bow, appeared around the edge of the doorway. Wearing too much rouge and pale orange lipstick, she beamed a smile before hopping out from behind the door and fully showing herself with a happy "Ta-da!"

The effect was… Well, it was daffodils. Odelia had dressed, head to toe, in daffodils, including heavy gold-and-enamel daffodil earrings that looked as if they weighed a ton and a white, daffodil-dotted dress worn over an equally voluminous orange shift. Backless yellow shoes with plastic daffodils standing two inches high on the toes completed the outrageous ensemble.

It was all so breathtakingly Odelia.

Refusing to be embarrassed for her dear aunt, Kaylie embraced Odelia and affectionately declared, "You look positively floral today, Auntie."

Odelia giggled as happily as any girl. "Thank you, dear. I love your penguins." She waved a lacy handkerchief in Stephen's direction, saying, "Looks like we both dressed in honor of our guest today."

Kaylie shot Stephen a desperate, pleading look. A moment passed, during which he gaped, before he realized what she wanted from him.

Proving that he had manners enough to be nice, he said to Odelia, "Uh, thanks. Very…clever."

"That outfit certainly puts you in mind of Holland,"

Kaylie supplied helpfully, "which is so well-known for its beautiful flowers."

"Oh, right," he managed, "especially tulips."

"Well, daffodils aren't tulips," Odelia said with a laugh, holding out her filmy white skirt, "as Magnolia pointed out to me at breakfast. And she would know." Leaning closer, the daffodil-clad Odelia confided to their guest, "She's a self-trained horticulturist, my sister is, almost a botanist, really. Loves her garden and greenhouse." Odelia smiled and turned to show off her finery. "But they're almost tulips, aren't they? Very like. And it's not as if there's a tulip dress in every closet, is it?"

Stephen opened his mouth but apparently found nothing to say in reply to that and so wound up simply shaking his head.

"Can we help you with something, Aunt Odelia?" Kaylie asked quickly.

"Oh, no, dear, not at all. Just checking on our Mr. Gallow. How is the dear boy?"

Biting her lip, Kaylie telegraphed an apologetic look to him then indulgently said to her aunt, "As well as can be expected. How kind of you to see about him."

"Kind," Stephen echoed, but he didn't fool Kaylie. She knew exactly what he was thinking. Kind of weird. Kind of ridiculous. Maybe even kind of loony.

"I'm going to be out later this afternoon," Kaylie said to Odelia, telling Stephen with her eyes that this was payback. "Maybe you could check in on him then."

Even while Stephen glared daggers at Kaylie, Odelia clapped her hands, hanky fluttering. "I have a lovely idea! Perhaps we'll take tea here with Mr. Gallow this afternoon."

Jerking, he looked for a moment as if he would spring off the bed and flee. Kaylie indulged in a smirk. As if he could outrun Odelia, even in her flip-flop daffodil shoes. Kaylie did have some pity for him, though. She knew how much he hated tea, and he was recovering from serious wounds, so she let him off the hook.

"I think the tea will have to wait until he's stronger."

"Oh, of course. Of course. Poor thing."

He did look terribly weary.

"I think we ought to let him rest now," she told her aunt.

"Well, I'll leave you then," Odelia said, turning away. "Just sing out if you need anything, Mr. Gallow."

"Yes, ma'am," he said. "Thanks. But it's Stephen, please. Or Steve, if you prefer."

Looking back at him over her shoulder, Odelia batted her eyelashes at him. "Stephen. Such an elegant name."

Elegantly named Stephen appeared to have a touch of dyspepsia. Odelia frilled her hanky at him in a coquettish wave and clacked away in her daffodil shoes.

Stephen and Kaylie looked at each other in silence until the clattering faded, at which point Stephen drolly observed, "There's a word for her in Dutch. It's 'kooky.'"

Kaylie flattened her lips in a flat, scolding line to keep from laughing. "That's not very nice."

"How about *zonderling,* then?"

She narrowed her eyes at him. "Meaning?"

"Eccentric."

Zonderling. Kaylie had to bite her lip to hold back a smile. "Why do you think we call her Auntie Od?" she said softly.

Stephen grinned. "Well, if the name fits…"

"She's also a complete sweetheart who cares about everyone and everything," Kaylie hastily defended, "and the reason you're here, by the way."

"She's the reason? How's that? I thought Dr. Leland arranged this."

"Brooks asked Aunt Odelia to open Chatam House to you,

and she did, but of course he knew she would. That's why he asked her in particular, I'm sure."

"And I suppose it had nothing to do with the very generous sum of money we offered," Stephen retorted.

"Which went to charity," Kaylie reminded him, leaning a shoulder against the footpost of the bed.

"Right," he said. "I support a lot of charities."

Kaylie smiled, strangely delighted to hear it. "Really? Which ones?"

"Whichever ones the team tells me to. It's in my contract. Pain in the, ah, you-know-what most of the time." He made a little shrug. "But that's how it is. Comes with the territory."

Deflated, Kaylie bowed her head. "That's nice." For a moment there, she'd thought she'd stumbled onto something that her father might appreciate about this man. Glancing at her wristwatch again, she saw that she was running late and pushed away from the footpost, saying briskly, "I have to go. Don't get up unless there's someone here to help you. All right?"

"Fine," Stephen muttered resentfully, laying his head back on the pillow.

He let out a gusty sigh. Kaylie paused for an instant, worried that he might be in more pain than she'd supposed, but then his eyes drifted shut and his big body seemed to relax. She realized that he would be asleep within moments.

Tiptoeing from the room, she pulled her keys from the pocket of her smock and headed downstairs. As she slid behind the wheel of her beloved convertible some minutes later, she shook her head. Imagine driving through the walls of a house and into a fireplace. The wonder that was Stephen hadn't been killed.

She thought of her father, waiting for her at home. No doubt, he would behave as petulantly and spoiled as the man she was leaving behind for his sake. It struck her suddenly how alike the two were. Stephen had survived a horrendous accident and would ultimately be none the worst for wear. Hub had survived a massive heart attack without damage to his heart muscle. Except for the medication that he must take to control his cholesterol and blood pressure, his life should have been little changed. Both had good reason to praise God; yet, both behaved as if God was picking on him. How could it be, she wondered, that two such different men—one of them an elderly retired Christian minister, the other a fierce, young, physical competitor—had so much in common?

"Are You trying to tell me something here, Lord?" she asked softly. *Is this my true calling, then?* she went on in silence. *Am I made to nurse fractious, unreasonable men? Or am I missing something?*

She wanted to help. She truly did. She wanted to help her father, and she wanted to help Stephen Gallow.

"Show me, Lord," she whispered. "Please show me what to do."

Chapter Five

As much as he disliked her being away from his side, Stephen had to admit that Kaylie proved as good as her word. She arrived back at Chatam House just after noon and brought up his lunch. Despite his nap, however, she wisely judged him too weak to make the trek back into the sitting room. She was right. He felt like a limp dishcloth; much as it grated, he dined in bed after only a token argument.

Later, she helped him clean up somewhat and change into fresh clothing, but he simply did not have the energy to shave. She decided to forego wrapping his ribs for the time being. For one thing, he wasn't likely to be doing much more moving around today. For another, his incisions were still sore to the touch. Eventually she dosed him with painkiller that he did not want but desperately needed. After disappearing into the bowels of the house with his lunch tray, she must have left again a short time later, for she was gone when he awakened in just over two hours.

Her aunts popped in and out during the afternoon, thankfully one at a time and sans tea tray. Stephen found them surprisingly entertaining.

Hypatia was the first. Graceful and slight, she put him in mind of the beloved queen of the Netherlands, Beatrix. She seemed to simply appear in the chamber, giving Stephen something of a start. He looked up from playing a game on his phone and there, without warning, she stood. Almost terrifyingly proper, she had him actually speaking in perfect syntax during their brief interview, as if he expected to be graded on his grammar. It didn't take long for him to realize that Hypatia reigned as the undisputed authority at Chatam House.

He was bored enough to have picked up a book when Magnolia clumped in bearing two vases of flowers, one of which she left atop the dresser in his bedroom. The other stayed in the sitting room. Frumpy and a tad on the stocky side, she seemed more than a little suspicious, sniffing the air as if checking for gas leaks. When he politely asked about the flowers, however, she eagerly told him more than he'd ever wanted to know about the various blossoms. How could he not describe the incredible tulip fields of Holland and the massive international flower market in Amsterdam for her? Afterward, to his disgust, he drifted off to sleep again, despite becoming surprisingly but thoroughly engrossed in a mystery novel with a floral theme, of all things.

Odelia woke him when she brought up his dinner, a succulent baked chicken breast and yams, with asparagus and pickled beets. Kaylie sailed in while they were trying to get situated and took over, allowing Odelia to leave in a flutter of lace and daffodils. Stephen gobbled down everything, including the beets, relieved to find his appetite strong and ridiculously glad to see Kaylie with her sweet smile and her hair windblown, tendrils escaping her ponytail to waft about her face. She admired the flower arrangements and teased him about Magnolia taking a liking to him. Frightening thought.

She helped him take care of his personal needs then stayed

to hold a small mirror while he used the electric razor that Aaron had supplied him at the hospital. She asked questions about the book he was reading and surprised him by saying that she would have to take a look at it herself once he had finished with it. Then she made him comfortable, administering his meds and straightening his bed with brisk, easy, efficient motions. Her placid smile remained fixed but somewhat impersonal.

That irked him for some reason, and the fact that he could not bully himself into staying awake long enough even to check the scores of the night's hockey games did not help. As the drug and his own exhaustion pulled him under, he thought unhappily that he should be playing tonight and instead may have tanked his career. To add insult to injury, his pretty little nurse apparently did not like him. God clearly felt the same.

Carrying such thoughts into sleep with him, he should not have been surprised that his rest was uneasy. Yet, when the nightmare came in the dark of the night, it took him unaware. One moment he floated in a vast, black sea of oblivion, then suddenly he found himself behind the wheel of the sleek, low-slung, midnight-blue sports car that had been his signing gift to himself. He had bought the vehicle as soon as the ink had dried on his first pro contract and couldn't wait to show it off. The valet at the club where he and Nick had stopped in for drinks earlier that evening had gushed about what a sweet ride it was when he'd delivered it to the curb that night and traded Stephen the keys for a generous tip.

Adrenaline pumped in Stephen's veins as he put the car through its paces. It sped through the night, wind whipping through the open windows, Nick whooping it up in the passenger seat. Pleased with life, Stephen laughed and stomped the gas pedal. Nick braced an arm against the dash, howling with glee as the car shot forward.

Suddenly headlights appeared. Stephen knew with sickening dread that he was dreaming and exactly what was coming, but he could do nothing.

"No! No!" he cried. "Wake up! Wake up!"

He tried everything, from trying to rouse himself from the dream to yanking and pounding the steering wheel, but nothing prevented the bone-jarring crash. Then they were rolling, banging around the interior of the car as it tumbled. Unbelted, Nick slammed into him more than once, tossed about like a rag doll. Stephen knew that the car would come to rest on the passenger side and what he would see then.

Blood. Shattered glass. Crumpled metal. Nick, twisted and broken.

Howling in grief, Stephen clawed at his own safety restraints. Abruptly, the colored lights of emergency vehicles flashed macabre shadows across the scene, but Stephen knew it was too late. Still, he struggled, sobbing and screaming, desperate to reach the dearest person in his world. Nick could not be gone. He could not, for how could anyone possibly live in a world without Nicklas?

The call came on the house phone, not the expensive mobile unit that Stephen Gallow had insisted she must have. Somehow, though, even as she reached for the receiver on the low chest beside her bed, Kaylie knew that it had to do with him. Hearing Odelia's trembling voice on the other end of the line only confirmed that assumption.

"Kaylie? Can you come? He's fallen, and the pain is terrible. We don't know what to do."

"I'll be right there," she answered without hesitation, throwing off the bedcovers.

Her father tapped on her bedroom door as she pulled on her scrubs. "One moment!" Reaching for the doorknob with one hand, she stuffed a pair of socks into a pocket with the other.

"What's going on?" Hub demanded, yanking a knot in the belt of his plaid robe. "I heard the phone ring, and it's not even 5:00 a.m."

"Stephen has fallen," she told him, stomping her bare feet into athletic shoes.

"Who is Stephen?"

"Mr. Gallow."

"Your new patient?"

"That's right."

Hubner rolled his eyes. "I knew this job would turn into a terrible imposition."

Kaylie tried to hang on to her patience as she stuffed her wallet into her pocket and grabbed her keys. "I don't have time to discuss it, Dad."

Pushing past him, she moved down the narrow hallway and into the living room. Hub padded along behind her in his house slippers.

"When will you be back?"

"I have no idea."

She skirted the room, with its comfortably worn furnishings and fieldstone fireplace. Just as she reached the opening to the small foyer, a lamp snapped on and her father spoke again.

"What about breakfast?" he asked, the faintest whine in his voice. "Will you be back in time to get breakfast, do you think?"

Exasperated, Kaylie rounded on him. "I don't know, Dad. Thankfully, you can feed yourself."

Something dark and troubling flashed across his face, but Kaylie's worry for Stephen pushed all other considerations away just then. She whirled and rushed out, telling herself that she would apologize later. As she raced toward Chatam House, her only prayer was for the injured man who had put that tremor into her auntie's voice.

Locking his jaw, Stephen held still as Kaylie injected medication into his upper right leg. Red-hot pain radiated up and down from the thigh, knifing up into his hip and down into the plaster cast below his knee, all the way to the ankle. Add to that the intense throbbing in his ribs, and it was all he could do retain consciousness.

Nevertheless, as soon as Kaylie recapped the syringe, he insisted through his teeth, "I do not need an ambulance!" For all the good that did him. She had already made the call to 9-1-1.

Ignoring his desires entirely, she turned to address those crowded into his bedroom. She surprised him, this small, wholesome, quiet woman; he might even have been fascinated by the cool, competent manner in which she had taken control and created order out of chaos within moments of her arrival, had she not ignored his every wish and order.

"Carol, would you go down and watch for the emergency vehicle, please?" she directed briskly. "Hilda, I think everyone is going to need a hot cup of tea soon."

Carol, in her messy ponytail and hastily donned slacks and blouse, nodded. Dressed in a threadbare caftan, her elder sister Hilda did the same. Her straight, thin, gray-dulled yellow-gold hair flopped about her double chin.

"I'll heat some cinnamon rolls, too." She went out with her younger sister.

Chester, wearing black pants and a white undershirt with bare feet, watched his wife and sister-in-law leave without comment, then looked to Kaylie for his own assignment.

"Thank you for helping to get him back into bed," she told the older man.

Stephen grunted in agreement. He wouldn't have believed that the old guy could manage it, but somehow he had, though at the time Stephen had thought the transfer from the floor to the bed would kill him. He'd have bitten off his own tongue before he'd have admitted it, of course. He was a hockey player, for pity's sake, toughest of the tough.

Kaylie dispatched Chester to move the sofa in the sitting room so the paramedics could get a gurney into the bedroom. He went out to rearrange furniture in his bare feet. That left just the aunts and Kaylie herself.

"What can we do, dear?" Odelia asked, looking like a runaway from the circus, with pink foam rubber curlers in her white hair and a ruffled, knee-length, red satin robe zipped over a floor-length yellow nylon gown. Stephen would have laughed if he hadn't been so busy trying not to whimper like a wounded dog.

Magnolia, her long braid intact, wore a flannel robe over flannel pajamas, while Hypatia, her silver hair clubbed sleekly at her nape, appeared ready to receive visitors in tailored navy silk with white piping. Her silent, intelligent gaze contained a good deal of concern, along with a measure of speculation that unnerved Stephen. She had been the first to arrive after his fall, and he sensed that she at least suspected the cause.

He closed his eyes to escape that acute amber gaze and heard Kaylie say, "Just pray for him. I'm pretty sure he's broken another bone above the leg cast and dislodged the old break."

Stephen felt the terrible urge to cry, partly because the leg screamed and partly because a really bad break could mean the end of his career. If so, he—and only he—could be blamed. He had done some stupid, stupid things in his life and would never, apparently, quit paying for them.

While silently berating himself, he felt the gentle touch of several hands on his shoulder and chest. He looked up to find the Chatam sisters standing over him, their heads bowed and eyes closed. A glance at Kaylie, who hugged the footpost of the bed, showed that she, too, stood in an attitude of prayer. Before he could digest the amazing notion that they were actually going to pray over him at that very moment, Hypatia began to speak.

"Father God, we entreat You, on behalf of this poor man. You know his great pain, Lord. You know the reasons for it. Give him comfort now, Father, please. Heal him inside and out. Let him feel Your great love and power. You have brought him here to this place for a reason, Lord, and we trust that it will work out for his best and Your great glory and honor. Make us blessings to that cause, Sovereign Father. These things we pray in the name of Your Holy Son and our Savior. Amen."

Stephen lay dumbfounded for several seconds before realizing that, to his utter shock, the pain seemed to have subsided to a manageable level. Oh, but surely that had more to do with the injection that Kaylie had administered moments ago than any prayer. Didn't it? If so, it would be the fastest working injection he had ever received, but then his sense of time was surely skewed.

Carol shouted up the stairwell that the ambulance had arrived, and Hypatia immediately went into action, herding her sisters from the room. "We had best get out of the way now. Kaylie can manage this." She paused at the bedside long enough to look down on Stephen again. "We will be praying for your swift return to us, Stephen dear. God bless."

Stephen dear. It felt suddenly as if he had unknowingly crossed some divide and managed to plant himself in the bosom of the Chatam family. Nameless emotion swelled his chest. Unaccustomed to such feelings, he attempted to turn it off with an icy glare, but for once his game face failed him. A tight smile curling up one corner of her mouth, Hypatia patted his shoulder comfortingly and followed her sisters from the room. Kaylie instantly took her place, bending low to sweep a lock of hair from his forehead and address him softly.

That absurd, nameless yearning swept through him again. Why, he wondered, did the slightest display of tenderness from this woman reduce him to a maudlin nostalgia for something he had never known and could not even describe? She was not his mother. She was not his girlfriend. She was not even his type. She was a paid nurse, an employee, an uptight little holy-roller with as much disapproval as pity in her big, dark eyes. Yet, something about her made him want more than simple professional comfort from her.

"Stephen, listen to me. I need to know how it happened."

A great clattering and thumping on the landing snagged his attention. "They're here."

"I know. Quickly. How did it happen? Why did you fall?"

He shook his head, unwilling to say. Hypatia might suspect, but she didn't *know*, and she wouldn't if he could help it. This was his issue, his secret shame. But then Kaylie gently cupped his face with her small, delicate hands, as if it, he, were somehow precious to her. He could not have denied her anything at that moment.

"It's important, Stephen. Please."

"Nightmare," he admitted tersely, shifting his gaze from hers.

"It's not the first, is it?" she whispered, her voice a sweet, soft zephyr of compassion. Her hands stroked his face, creating an island of bliss in a sea of pain and angst.

Men and material suddenly crowded the room. Kaylie left him to sweep all of his medications from his bedside table into the pockets of her smock and answer questions from the emergency medical technicians. Two of them moved into position and quickly transferred him from the bed to the gurney, an excruciating experience that Stephen endured with a clenched jaw.

The trip out of the suite, down the stairs and into the ambulance was every bit as painful as he'd expected. He gulped and gritted his teeth, training his gaze on the frescoed ceiling above, a painting of blue sky, fluffy cloud and feathers. Suddenly a large, ornate crystal chandelier blocked the peaceful scene.

Stephen closed his eyes and attempted to blank his mind, only to find Hypatia's prayer whispering inside his head. *Give him comfort now, Father, please. Heal him inside and out. Let him feel Your great love and power.* Before he knew what he was doing, Stephen was adding his own plea to Hypatia's prayer. *I know I don't deserve it, but please, please help me.*

He felt an odd sensation sweep through him, a chill that was not cold, a wind that did not blow. Then suddenly the EMTs were loading the gurney into the ambulance. To his horror, Stephen heard a man's voice say, "Good grief. That's Hangman Gallow. What's the star goalie of the Blades hockey team doing here in Buffalo Creek?"

Stephen groaned. So much for prayer and keeping a low profile! The news of his whereabouts would likely be splashed all over the DFW Metroplex by evening, and speculation about his accident would soon run rampant. Team management would probably be screaming in Aaron's ear before week's end. As if reading his thoughts, Kaylie clambered up into the ambulance with him, clasped his good hand with hers and spoke into his ear.

"Don't worry. These are medical personnel bound by privacy laws, but I'll speak to them myself just to be sure that nothing slips out."

He doubted that it would make any difference. He was going to lose it all anyway. Deep down, he'd always known it, but he'd keep fighting to the very end, because that's what he did, he fought. Always.

"Never give up," he muttered.

Drugs, weariness and pain all weighed on him, pushing him down toward oblivion, but he struggled to stay awake, to stay in control.

"I can do this," he told himself, trying to believe that he could survive yet another setback. He had already survived more pain, disappointment and loss than many people knew in a lifetime. But this…this could be the end.

"It's all right," a voice whispered. "Just relax."

For a moment, he was confused. Was that his mother's voice? Aunt Lianna's? No, of course not. She hadn't spoken to him since Nick's death.

A man's deep voice said, "Doesn't look like he's been doing too well."

Stephen roused, wondering when his father had come. "I'll do better," he vowed. "I'm not a pansy," he insisted, shaking his head. "Not a mama's boy. I can do it."

"Yes," said that sweet voice in his ear. "You can do it. You are doing it. Rest now. Just rest." Gentle hands pushed him down. Relief swept through him.

Rest. He could rest now. Tomorrow was soon enough to get back on his skates. Tomorrow he would prove himself. Again. But first, he would rest. Gratefully, he sank into unconsciousness.

When he woke again—it might have been minutes or hours later—they were off-loading him from the ambulance, and Kaylie Chatam was there, her small, delicate, feminine hand clasping his.

"I was dreaming," he muttered.

The smile that she rained down on him warmed every tiny corner of his heart.

"I know," she said sweetly. "I know. We're going to do something about that."

A pair of shapeless green scrubs and a working knowledge of the local hospital granted a gratifying amount of access in a process that might otherwise have relegated Kaylie to the role of distant observer. Instead, she'd been allowed to accompany Stephen in the ambulance. His mutterings had broken her heart, but she didn't have time to really think about what they had revealed.

As promised, she spoke to the EMT crew before they departed for their station, making it clear how important confidentiality was in this instance. They joked that they would avoid risking their careers for the price of autographs.

"Sure, sure," Stephen responded groggily. "Game tickets even."

"But later," she insisted to a quartet of smiling male faces. "We'll be in touch."

Thankfully, no one questioned her right to stay at Stephen's side. The emergency room physician was too concerned with Stephen's physical condition to care about such things. He was not someone Kaylie knew well, but he seemed to accept her presence without question and allowed her to provide the necessary information pertaining to previous injuries and prescription drugs.

No one said a contrary word when she accompanied Stephen to X-ray, not even when she squeezed into the lead-shielded operations niche with the technician or studied the developed pictures. Every time she returned to Stephen's side, his hand groped for hers, and she always gave it to him, understanding well that she had become, by sheer default, his lifeline in this situation.

While they waited for the doctor to report his findings, Stephen blearily asked her to tell him what to expect. She could have put him off with medical mumbo jumbo or disclaimers about her personal expertise, but she chose instead to give him the truth.

"I think you're looking at surgery, Stephen. There's a new break above the cast, and the old break appears to have been dislocated. It looked to me like you have some fragmenting there. That sometimes means a shortening of the bone."

What color remained in his face drained away, and the grip on her fingers became almost punishing. "So it really could be the end of everything," he rumbled.

"Of course it's not the end of everything," she told him firmly. "Many people naturally have one leg that's slightly longer than the other. Most don't even know it. Few doctors even try to treat it if the discrepancy is less than three centimeters."

"Three centimeters," he echoed hollowly. "As little as three centimeters and I might never skate again. Oh, God."

"At least you're looking in the right direction for help," Kaylie told him, bending close and smiling indulgently. She was discovering that the man beneath the tough exterior had fears and concerns like any other and that he responded to a compassionate touch with a silent, secret hunger that clutched at her heart. "Would you like to pray about it?"

His gray eyes, foggy and bleak now, plumbed hers. "I—I don't think I know how. I have tried. I even learned a prayer once, but…"

"What is it? What prayer did you learn?"

He stared at her for a moment then squeezed his eyes shut and whispered, "Our Father, Who art in heaven."

"Hallowed be thy name," Kaylie joined in, repeating the familiar words of the Lord's Prayer with him. At the end, she added her own. "Please, Lord, if it can be within Your will, spare Stephen the loss of his skating. Surely You have given him the talent and desire to play hockey for a reason. Show him what that reason is, to Your glory. Amen."

"Amen," he whispered.

A throat cleared, and Kaylie turned to find that the doctor had once more entered the cubicle. She gripped Stephen's hand and waited for the verdict.

Surgery. Kaylie was right about that.

Please, God, Stephen thought, *let her be right about everything else.*

He almost laughed at himself. Praying at the drop of a hat now, was he? As if God had ever listened to him! The Chatams, on the other hand, when Kaylie or her aunts prayed, it was as if they summoned the very presence of God into the room, as if that Power drew close and cloaked them in peace.

Stephen knew that he had clung to Kaylie all that morning like a toddler clinging to a security blanket, but he couldn't seem to help himself. Thankfully, she didn't appear to mind. More than likely, she considered it a part of her job, so he hesitated only a moment before asking if she would be there with him during the surgery.

She tilted her head, her long, sleek, dusky red hair sliding freely about her face and shoulders. He caught his breath. With her hair down around her clean face and those big dark eyes glowing with concern, she looked too beautiful to be of this earth. Only the presence of the doctor and the entry of another nurse into the room kept Stephen from foolishly reaching up to clasp the nape of Kaylie's neck and pull her down to him for a kiss.

"I'm sorry," she told him softly. "The operating room is one place I cannot go, but I'll be right here, praying for you."

Stephen gulped and nodded. Then, as if aware of that longed-for kiss, she bent and pressed her lips to the center of his forehead. A sense of peace and well-being filled him. It flowed into the all the dark, lonely crevices of his soul, bringing light and something else along with it, something he had a difficult time identifying.

Hope, he decided woozily.

Not the hope for any one thing, but the mere chance, the opportunity, that something in his life might finally go right, that it might all somehow come together finally.

The feeling was almost embarrassingly intimate and, at the same time, comfortingly ordinary. It somehow set him apart from, yet united him with, all humanity. It elated and terrified. In an instant, the whole world and his perspective of it shifted from one of disappointment and struggle to one of teeming possibilities. He couldn't bear the thought that it might be imaginary, ethereal, fleeting, and in his clumsy way he attempted to grab on to it.

"Hey," he teased, swirling a finger around his forehead, "let's skip the meds from now on and just go with that. What do you say?"

Kaylie laughed and stepped back. Only then did he realize that he was about to be wheeled away. An orderly and an orthopedic surgeon had been summoned and an operating room cleared for immediate use, he was told.

"A smaller hospital sometimes has its benefits," Kaylie said.

Stephen nodded and reached out to her as he rolled past. She brushed his fingertips with hers.

"I know Dr. Philem personally, and he's one of the best orthopedists around," she assured him, keeping pace with the head of the gurney as it traveled down the gleaming corridor.

"Don't worry about a thing," she went on softly, "not even the nightmares. I think we can even take care of those."

Nightmares.

With that one word, she destroyed the first truly bright moment he had known in years. The nightmares unlocked all his horrors, all his failures, all his fears. All his guilt. As her face receded from his view, the all too familiar black pit of despair, disappointment and shame opened inside him, swallowing whole his momentary joy.

For what could possibly ever "take care of" the fact that he had killed his best friend?

Chapter Six

Rubbing her arms lightly, Kaylie studied the displays on a variety of machines surrounding Stephen's bed.

"So how is he?" Aaron asked, nervously jiggling the coins in the pocket of his light gray slacks.

"He's fine. They used a temporary nerve block so he'll probably feel better than he has in some time once he comes out from under the anesthesia."

Aaron had arrived just after the surgeon had given Kaylie the post-op summary. Brooks Leland, at the behest of the aunties, had contacted the personable sports agent, something Kaylie should have thought to do herself. Instead, for nearly two hours she had sat in the waiting room with her head bowed and her hands clasped, beseeching God on Stephen's behalf and thinking about what he had said in the ambulance and the way he had prayed with her before they'd taken him into surgery. That prayer had pricked her heart, a heart already softened by his physical suffering, mindless mutterings and the way in which his hand had repeatedly and continuously clasped hers. Perhaps Stephen was not a believer, but she had to believe that God was moving in Stephen's life.

Kaylie felt genuine delight at that, but she felt only sadness about what his words in the ambulance had revealed. Someone, she very much feared, had taunted Stephen as a child, called him a pansy and a mama's boy. Was that, she wondered, why he had chosen such a violent, punishing sport?

"What kind of cast is that?" Aaron asked, indicating the black casing that covered Stephen's leg from the hip to the ankle, leaving the sole of his foot bare.

Pulled from her reverie, Kaylie explained that in a few weeks the temporary cast, along with the screws that the surgeon had inserted to stabilize the bone, would be removed and replaced with a cast that would allow Stephen to walk, or at least get around on his own somewhat. The recovery-room nurse—a brisk, plump, forty-something woman whose name Kaylie could not recall—breezed into the curtained cubicle while Kaylie continued to answer Aaron's questions about this latest mishap and the doctor's prognosis.

After a moment, Kaylie heard the woman say, "Mr. Gallow? Mr. Gallow, can you hear me?"

Steven cleared his throat just as Kaylie turned back to the bed. "Yes," he croaked. "Where'm I?"

"You're in recovery, Stephen," Kaylie answered.

His eyes popped open, and he looked straight up into Kaylie's face, smiling crookedly. "'Lo, beautiful."

Instantly, his lids dropped closed again, and he went off on a sigh. Her heart lurching, Kaylie stepped back as the nurse went about checking his vital signs. Kaylie prayed that her face did not show the thrill that she had felt at his slurred compliment. The man was drugged, for pity's sake, and probably used to flirting with every other woman he saw. That's what sports stars did, wasn't it?

"Can you cough for me?" the nurse asked Stephen. His head rolled on the pillow, but he obliged, opening his eyes again.

"The two of you should go on up to his room now," the nurse said to Kaylie and Aaron. "We'll bring him to you as soon as he's ready."

"Wait, wait," Stephen mumbled, reaching out his good hand to Kaylie. "My leg. How many cen'meters?"

"None," she assured him, resisting the urge to clasp his fingers. Somehow, with her heart still tripping, it did not seem wise just then. "You lost no bone. The doctor was able to stabilize everything. It's going to take several weeks longer to heal than it might have otherwise, but it will heal."

Stephen breathed out a huge sigh of relief, dropped his head back on the pillow and mumbled, "Keep th' prayers comin', *liefje.*"

Aaron chuckled. "You just do what this nurse tells you. *Liefje.* See you up in your room."

Stephen looked around in surprise at the sound of Aaron's voice. "Hey," he said through a big, goofy grin. "What're you doing here?"

"Looking at a trussed turkey." Aaron waved a hand in jocular farewell and turned away with Kaylie to start down the wide aisle between the rows of beds. "What am I doing here? As if I haven't always been here for him. Is he really going to be all right? He hasn't done himself in this time?"

"He's going to be just fine," Kaylie said, smacking a big round button on the wall that opened the wide mechanical doors at the end of the aisle. Her relief, however, was tempered by an uncomfortable feeling of having wandered onto dangerous territory.

As they ambled through those doors and into a bright corridor, Kaylie told herself that comforting the man and becoming emotionally involved with him were two different things. She would do well to remain as personally aloof as

possible for a number of reasons. For one, the man was obviously self-destructive. For another, he did not share her
faith. Thirdly, his lifestyle was utterly foreign to her. Spurred
by that, another thought occurred.

"What does *liefje* mean?" Kaylie asked after a moment.
She'd first thought that Stephen had merely mangled her name
due to his drug intoxication, but then Aaron had repeated the
word back to him in that teasing manner of his.

Aaron shot her a knowing, lopsided grin. "Sweetheart. It
means sweetheart."

Sweetheart. Kaylie's heart thunked. She felt a disturbing
shiver of delight, which was pure foolishness, of course. It
meant nothing to him, and should mean nothing to her.

"Hey, I've picked up a lot of the Dutch, you know," the
bluff agent went on, swaggering a bit.

"I'm sure," Kaylie muttered with a limp smile.

"I'm pretty good at stuff like that," he bragged. "Stevie,
now..." Aaron wagged a finger at her. "Stevie's good at two
things—hockey and hockcy. Everything else, like life, for
instance, well, he just never has seemed to get the hang of it."

Kaylie felt her heart sink. It was no more than she had suspected, of course. Mentally shaking her head, she sternly told
herself to get her mind back to business. What was wrong with
her anyway? She had allowed the mutterings of a drugged
patient to set her thoughts on a path that they would never have
wandered down otherwise. She chalked it up to exhaustion.
Losing several hours' sleep plus several hours of stress must
have scrambled her brain.

She suddenly wanted to go home. And why shouldn't she?
Stephen was out of surgery and would be spending the next
twenty-four to forty-eight hours in the hospital. Aaron was
here to lend support; she was no longer needed. Pushing aside

memories of how Stephen had clutched her hand earlier, she walked Aaron to the elevator, where she checked her watch. The time was just after 11:00 a.m.

"Listen," she said, punching the up button for him. "I'm going to swing by and give my aunts a brief report on Stephen, and then I have to get home to make lunch for my father."

Aaron blinked, obviously surprised. "But you're Steve's nurse."

"Aaron, he's in the hospital. He doesn't need a private nurse in the hospital."

"Uh-huh. Well, I have this sneaking suspicion that he's going to expect to see you, anyway."

"Tell him I'll be by tomorrow to check on him," she decided, backing away.

Aaron raised both eyebrows. A ding signaled the arrival of the elevator. Aaron spread his hands as the doors slid open. "Okay, then. Say hello for me to the old…uh, your aunts."

Kaylie nodded and made a little wave before turning and swiftly walking away. Stephen, she told herself, would be just fine, and she would be…

Safe? From what? Temptation?

Obviously, she would do well to keep her distance for now. Tomorrow, she would reestablish a professional relationship, and that would be that.

Meanwhile, her father undoubtedly needed mollifying. She regretted now the manner in which she had left him that morning. He had come to depend on her, after all, and she had impatiently blown him off. Yes, the situation had been an emergency, but now the crisis had passed.

It was time to get back to her real life and let God work in both situations—without her silly overreactions getting in the way.

* * *

"You really didn't have to come," Stephen said to Aaron, settling into the bed. *Another day, another bed,* he thought with a sigh. He was heartily sick of this state of affairs, but at least he wasn't in pain. Oddly, the leg throbbed but it didn't hurt. How weird was that?

"Hey, I had to be sure my meal ticket didn't get punched," Aaron said, shaking a finger at Stephen. "I've still got a few more meals in you."

"Right," Stephen drawled. It was a little late for Aaron to pretend that his only interest in Stephen was financial. "I appreciate it, man. I really do, but Kaylie says it's going to be all right, so you really didn't have to come all this way. Kaylie will take care of things here."

Aaron hunched a shoulder, a grim look on his face. "Yeah, well, she's going to be taking care of them from a distance then."

"What do you mean?"

"She ran along home to daddy. He needs his lunch."

Stephen frowned then told himself not to be ridiculous. "She'll be back after she gets him fed."

"I wouldn't count on it," Aaron told him. "She said to tell you she'd see you tomorrow."

"Tomorrow?" Confused and sluggish, Stephen shook his head. She hadn't left his side all morning, and she had to know that he'd already come to depend on her. "I don't get it."

Aaron brushed back the sides of his suit jacket and grinned, his hands parked at his waist. "Couldn't have anything to do with 'beautiful *liefje.*' Nah."

"Huh?"

"You don't remember calling her beautiful or *liefje?*"

He did, actually, but it had seemed perfectly natural at the time. Using his good hand, he rubbed the top of his head. "No big deal. I—I was dopey. Right?"

"Right. Don't worry about it," Aaron advised, still grinning. "I'm just gigging you. Nurse Dear isn't exactly your style. Right? Besides, it's like she said, you don't need a private nurse in the hospital."

That had not been Stephen's experience. The longer he'd been hospitalized before, the greater difficulty he'd had getting the nurses to respond to him, but he said nothing. No reason to give Aaron more ammunition.

"Say, speaking of Kaylie, she tells me that the paramedics who brought you in are expecting autographs," Aaron said.

Stephen nodded. "Yeah, I, uh, may even have promised them game tickets."

"Hey, if it'll keep them quiet…" Aaron shrugged.

Stephen agreed. Kaylie had said they wouldn't talk, that they were bound by privacy rules the same as her, but it didn't hurt to be accommodating. Besides, he owed them.

"I've got some autographed pucks out in the car," Aaron went on. "I'll bring some in before I leave. Okay? It's not like you can sign anything with your writing hand in a cast, after all."

"Always prepared," Stephen said with as much smile as he could muster. "So how did it go with the team last night?"

Aaron jingled the change in his pocket. "They lost, five to four."

Bad news. Or good, depending on how he wanted to look at it. He had a hard time thinking of it as good, even if it might mean that the team was missing him. "How's Kapimsky doing?"

Kapimsky was his replacement in the net, the young, untried backup goalie for the Blades.

Aaron shrugged. "Like you'd expect, stiff and nervous."

That would change, Stephen knew, with experience. The pressure-cooker of the playoffs was a tough place to get that experience, though. Winning the Stanley Cup was the goal of all thirty NHL teams, the be-all and end-all of pro hockey. For a team to advance to the Stanley Cup series, they had to win four of seven games in each of three rounds of finals. The two teams not eliminated at the end of those three rounds, one team from each division, would then battle for the cup with another series of seven games.

If the Blades advanced, management might start thinking young Kapimsky could handle the job and exercise the clause in Stephen's contract that allowed him to be cut. On the other hand, if the team lost, they might blame Stephen for not being in the net when they needed him most. Either way, it looked like a lose-lose proposition for him.

Still, he had gotten the team to their first playoff position. The franchise was only four years old, and he'd been guarding net for them for three. That had to count for something. If not, at least the possibility existed that he would be able to play elsewhere next season.

He wondered how much Kaylie's prayers had to do with that, but then he turned off that line of thought. He didn't want to think of Kaylie or her God just now. Her absence smarted in a way that he didn't want to examine too closely. It would pass. In all likelihood, it was nothing more than a result of his debilitated condition, anyway. That didn't keep it from stinging, a circumstance he found completely unacceptable.

After everything else that had happened, he knew better than to open himself up to that kind of disappointment. Especially now, with all he was currently going through and his future hanging in the balance, the last thing he needed was an emotional involvement. All he needed was a nurse. And peace. What, he wondered, made him think that he could have both in one small, wholesomely pretty woman?

"Aunt Hypatia, I'm sorry, but I'm bound by ethics and regulations. I can't discuss any specifics concerning my patient. I just wanted to let you know that Ste…Mr. Gallow's injuries and pain have been addressed."

"Well, of course, they have," Hypatia said with a sniff, waving her teacup at the other occupants of the sunroom. "That's what hospitals—and nurses—are for, and I understand that you have professional limitations, dear. My question is about his nightmares. *Do* you have any idea what is behind them?"

Kaylie shifted uncomfortably on the round seat of the high-backed, barrel-shaped rattan chair. "Ah, it's possible that the cause relates to his medical care."

Actually, inducing nightmares was a known side effect of at least one of Stephen's—Mr. Gallow's—pain medications. She probably should have mentioned that possibility to the doctors today, but it hadn't seemed as important as making sure that Stephen received the proper diagnosis and treatment for his injuries. If she had stayed, she most definitely would have asked that a notation to that effect be put in his chart, but tomorrow would surely be soon enough to mention it. The staff at the hospital, who had a complete list of his medications, would not give him the suspect drug while he was using intravenous painkillers anyway, so she really had no reason to feel guilty for leaving him. Yet, she did.

Hypatia set aside her teacup, making an uncharacteristically unladylike snort. "The cause relates to some trauma in that young man's past."

"Rooted in an unhappy childhood, no doubt," Odelia said, clasping her hands together, a lace hanky caught between them. "Oh, that poor dear boy." She was dressed almost solemnly today in a double-breasted, royal-blue pantsuit with gold buttons and earrings the size of small saucers. Kaylie could imagine demitasse cups sitting in their centers. Still, for

Odelia, this was positively funereal, especially as compared to the backdrop.

The sunroom at the rear of the house was a large, glassed-in space right next to the kitchen. Filled with pieces of bamboo and wicker furniture upholstered in a vivid floral pattern, it was a bright, restful space. A ceiling fan rotating lazily overhead stirred the fronds of palms and ferns scattered artfully about the room in large pots.

"There is more," Magnolia pronounced thoughtfully, munching on a gingersnap, "to our young Stephen than meets the eye."

Smiling wanly, Kaylie said nothing, glad that professional strictures prevented her from mentioning to her aunts what Stephen had said in the ambulance. It would only confirm their assumptions. On the other hand, their concern for him was genuine.

Hypatia sighed. "We'll just have to continue praying for him as best we can."

"I'm sure he'll appreciate that," Kaylie said, rising to her feet. "Now I'd better get home. Dad is probably anxious. I just wanted to check in with you."

"And when will you see Stephen again?" Odelia wanted to know.

"Sometime tomorrow."

"Give him our very best wishes," Magnolia said.

"And tell him," Odelia chirped, "that his room here is waiting for him."

"I will. It shouldn't be long before he's back," Kaylie assured her. "Day after tomorrow at the latest, I imagine."

"Yes, they don't keep anyone in the hospital very long these days," Hypatia said disapprovingly.

Kaylie let that go and passed out farewell kisses. "In case

I haven't told you," she said, on her way out of the room, "I admire what you're doing for Stephen."

"Oh, we're thrilled to do it," Odelia trilled, causing her sisters to aim very pointed looks at her. Subsiding into a meager smile, she waved her hanky at Kaylie, who went out mentally chuckling to herself.

She marveled that the sisters had agreed to take in an injured professional hockey player who was a complete stranger to them, but surely the whole thing had been directed by the caring hands of God.

"This is no good to me!"

Kaylie heard Stephen's voice raised in anger even before she pushed through the heavy door to his room early the next morning. A dark-haired nurse in violet scrubs straightened from a bent position and turned. She had a folded newspaper in her hands and an exasperated expression on her face, a face that Kaylie knew well.

"Hi, Linda. Problems?"

Linda Shocklea was an old schoolmate and a fine nurse. She rolled her eyes at the bed, flourishing the newspaper. "His Highness asked for a newspaper. I brought him a newspaper."

"There are no hockey scores in that local rag!" Stephen snapped. "I need a *real* newspaper."

Linda slapped the offending paper under her arm, saying, "I have explained that the local paper is all we get delivered up here and I cannot leave my post to go downstairs to find him a Fort Worth or Dallas paper."

Stephen ignored her, gesturing heatedly toward the television mounted high in one corner of the room. "They don't even have a sports channel on the TV!"

Kaylie smiled apologetically at the other nurse. "I've been hired to care for Mr. Gallow. Leave this to me."

Heaving a relieved sigh, Linda pulled open the door. "Gladly."

Obviously, Stephen had been making a nuisance of himself. Kaylie turned to face her employer, her hands linked together at her waist. For a long moment, he would not meet her gaze, just sat there in the bed fuming.

And to think, Kaylie mused, *that I had such a difficult time staying away last night.*

It hadn't helped that her father had been in such a surly mood. He had started out sounding concerned and solicitous, his earlier pique ameliorated by his delight that she had returned home in time to see to his lunch. He had even asked about Stephen's condition. She had answered as well as she was able, mindful of Stephen's privacy concerns. The problem had come when her father's queries had turned to Stephen himself, or, more to the point, when she had answered them, particularly the question about Stephen's age.

"So young?" her father had said, frowning. "I thought Mr. Gallow to be an elderly individual."

She had been somewhat taken aback by that, but even more so by her father's rapidly darkening mood. By dinner, she had resorted to keeping out of her father's way, and she had quickly found herself thinking that she could serve better at the hospital. But she had stayed at home, judging it the wiser action. Evidently, she had been right to come this morning, however, rather than wait until the afternoon.

"I'll go down and get you a paper," she told Stephen quietly.

He folded his arms mulishly. The gesture lost something due to the fact that his left arm was already bent at the elbow, set in a cast and strapped to his chest. She disciplined a smile. Suddenly his hand shot out.

"Forget the paper. Give me your phone. I'll look up the scores on the Internet."

"No," she said calmly, "you can't."

His face, already shadowed with two days' growth of beard, darkened. "Why not? I bought that phone. I can use it if I want."

"Cell phone use is strictly forbidden in patient and treatment areas, no matter who owns the phone."

He glared at her, slapped the heel of his hand against his forehead and literally growled. "Raaaaagggh!"

"I'll go now so I can get back before the doctors make their rounds," she said.

"Fine," he snapped. "Go. Go! You're good at that."

That hit home. Obviously, he had missed her yesterday. She didn't know whether to be pleased or troubled. Ducking her head, she quietly slipped from the room. Hurrying down to the gift shop, she picked up both the Dallas and the Fort Worth papers, then swiftly returned to Stephen's room. He seemed somewhat mollified when she handed over the newspapers. At least he didn't bite her hand.

Digging through the pile, he found the sports section of one paper and clumsily began spreading it out on the bed. Kaylie stepped in and turned the pages for him until he found what he wanted. Then she folded the paper, with the story exposed, and placed it in his good hand. He read earnestly for several minutes. Finally, he closed his eyes and let his head fall back on the pillow.

"You're pleased," she said, smiling as a warm glow filled her chest. It seemed ridiculous to feel so delighted at evidence of his pleasure, but she couldn't help herself. He thrust the paper at her. Taking that as an order to read it, she did so. From what she could gather, the team had lost the first game of a series, despite some excellent penalty killing and other things she didn't understand. Finally, she hit upon the paragraph that she thought might have so pleased Stephen.

"Most said it would be enough for this young team to make it to the playoffs for the first time in their short history," she read aloud. "Today, despite this loss out of the starting gate, expectations are building. The one flaw in that scenario is the position of goalie. Abel Kapimsky, 24, is a promising young goaltender and shows flashes of pure brilliance, but he's no Stephen Gallow. Then again, who in this conference is?"

She went on to read in silence how Gallow's goaltending had lifted the general level of play for the whole team and been instrumental in winning that first playoff berth. The writer noted that the mysterious injury which had taken Gallow out of the lineup could have also taken the wind out of the team's sails. That, to the team's credit, had not happened. After the loss, the team captain had, in fact, admonished his team to go out there and win the next one for the Hangman.

Smiling, Kaylie tossed the paper onto the bed. "Well," she said blithely, "that ought to lighten your mood."

Those gray eyes tried to freeze her where she stood. "I have good reason for my mood."

"Mmm, and I suppose the same goes for your attitude," she ventured softly. Those icy eyes narrowed, but for some reason Kaylie found herself smiling.

"What's wrong with my attitude?"

"Oh, please. A little honesty, now."

"Meaning?"

"Has no one ever told you that you can catch more flies with honey than vinegar?"

"Has no one ever told you that you look better with your hair down?" he sniped.

Kaylie's hand went automatically to the heavy twist of

hair at her nape. She almost always confined it when she was working. Otherwise, it got in the way. Self-consciously, she dropped the hand, dismayed to find that her first impulse had been to dig out the pins and clips that maintained the chignon. She didn't know what was worse—that he thought her unattractive with her hair confined or that she cared what he thought about her looks.

"Sorry," Stephen muttered, having the grace to shoot her a sheepish glance. "You look fine. I only meant that you have gorgeous hair. How you wear it is none of my business."

He thought she had gorgeous hair! Her hand once more sneaked up to touch the offending chignon, and she quickly turned away, unwilling to let him see how much his opinion affected her. "Thank you," she murmured, trying not to feel too pleased.

"I said I'm sorry, all right?" he grumbled.

Nodding, she bent to check the drip rate on his intravenous unit. "No problem."

"Arrrgh!"

She turned to find him beating his fist against his forehead. Alarmed, she asked, "Are you in pain?"

He dropped his hand, glaring at her. "No, I'm not in pain. Not much, anyway. I am in a foul mood. I admit it. Okay? I hate hospitals, and I hate not being able to get out of this bed! I'm bored out of my gourd and I'm worried—" He broke off.

"Worried about your career," she surmised.

"Wouldn't you be?" he shot back.

Kaylie didn't bother answering that. Instead, she sent up a silent prayer as she sifted through the second newspaper on the bed. Finding the sports section, she thumbed through it until she came to the hockey report. Quickly scanning the article, she saw that this reporter was not nearly as sanguine about the loss and the team's chances, for one pertinent reason. Reading aloud from the article, she pitched her voice to a strong, authoritative level.

"As thrilled as the fans may be at the team's long overdue entry into the playoffs, the hope of the Blades began and ended with goalie Stephen Gallow, who has had his problems off the ice in the past but rarely on it. Hurry back, Hangman! We need you."

She looked up in time to catch a look of raw emotion on his face. It was an expression of relief and pride and abject longing. Understanding struck. In an instant, she saw what Stephen Gallow would likely never admit even to himself, that like everyone else in this world, deep down, he needed to be needed. That's what playing for the Blades was really about for him. He just wanted someone to need him. She, who had felt the needs of so many and counted them a burden, felt suddenly ashamed.

Chapter Seven

Folding the paper neatly, Kaylie passed it to Stephen for his own perusal. He seemed to soak in every word. A faint smile curved his lips, but the face that he presented to her clearly showed concern.

"This helps, but sports writers and team management are not the same."

"No, they're not," she agreed, "but neither one is God. Why don't you leave the future to Him and concentrate on getting well?"

"Easy for you to say," Stephen muttered, looking at the article again.

"Yes," she said meaningfully. "Yes, it is." When he made no response to that, she changed the subject. "When's the next game?"

The frown came back to Stephen's face. "Tomorrow night." He glared at the television in the corner. The folded sheet of newspaper dropped to the bed. "You think there's any chance I can get out of here before then?"

Kaylie smiled. "We'll see what the doctors say."

"It helps that I have you, right?" he pressed, sitting up a

little straighter. The pillow slid down behind him, and Kaylie reached around to pull it back up. "I mean, you can take care of me at home, uh, Chatam House, so why stay here? Yeah?"

"We'll see," she repeated, smiling.

Stephen leaned back. "I need you, you know." Kaylie blinked, more than merely surprised. "No, really. Yesterday, for instance. What would I have done without you?"

"Someone would have called an ambulance," she told him.

"Yeah, maybe, but who would have held my hand throughout one of the worst days of my life?"

She said nothing to that, but when he held out his hand, she placed her own in it.

"I need you, Kaylie," he said softly. "That's why it's so tough when you cut out on me."

Warmth spread throughout her chest, radiating from her heart. "I'll do my best for you, Stephen," she told him, "I promise you, my very best. But I do have other obligations, you know. My dad needs me, too."

His smile flattened. "Sure," he said, letting go of her hand. He glanced around the room. "So what now? We stare at the walls until the docs show up?"

Sighing, Kaylie gathered up the newspapers. "Why don't we start by taking a look at the news?"

"Oh, that'll cheer me right up," he grumbled, but he lay there and listened to her read, commenting from time to time and offering reasoned, if sometimes sarcastic, arguments when she disagreed with him. In truth, they agreed more often than not, and Kaylie found some of his comments to be surprisingly insightful, informed, no doubt, by his life on two continents.

His foul mood seemed to lighten considerably, and his pain level remained low. The nerve block administered by the surgeon would wear off sometime in the next thirty-six to forty-eight hours, and his pain would return to previous levels, but she trusted that they could manage it successfully. Though mercurial, Stephen in a better mood and not in pain was a delightful experience, and it pleased her to be responsible for that in some small way.

Perhaps it pleased her too much.

"In the Netherlands," Stephen pointed out in response to an article on highway gridlock, "if you live more than ten kilometers from your job—that's just over six miles—your employer must provide you with a bicycle."

"A bicycle!" Kaylie exclaimed. "Oh, yeah, that would work. I can just see it now, bicycles fighting all those pickup trucks for space on our freeways. Yikes!"

"The bicycles don't go on the freeways," Stephen pointed out. "They go on the city streets, which have special bike lanes, and that frees up space on the highway."

"Bike lanes aside—and I've never seen a bike lane on a Texas street—what about heat stroke? We get triple-digit summers here, not to mention other extreme weather."

"The weather's not the issue. They get freezing weather in the Netherlands. The issue is distance. Here, everybody lives an hour's drive from work."

"Not everyone can live where they work," she argued.

He started to reply, but just then the door swooshed open and Brooks Leland strode into the room. Tall and fit with a touch of distinguished gray at his temples, a stethoscope about his neck and a white, knee-length lab coat in place of a suit jacket, the general practitioner was both genial and handsome. Stephen had liked Leland from the first moment they'd met only days earlier, but the instant the other man's eyes lit on Kaylie, Stephen knew the good doctor's likeability was about to take a nosedive.

The plummet began when Kaylie hopped up from the bedside chair and rushed toward Leland, calling out, "Brooks!"

It dropped like a rock when the doctor grinned and opened his arms. "There's my favorite nurse."

The two didn't just embrace, they hugged, rocking side to side in their exuberance.

"Kaylie darlin'," Brooks Leland drawled, pulling back slightly to gaze down at her, "it's been too long."

"That's what you get for being such a stranger," she scolded playfully. "Why don't you ever come by anymore? Dad would love to see you."

"I'll make a point of it. Soon."

"You better."

The door opened again, bumping Leland in the back, and another white coat slipped into the room. Stephen recognized the orthopedic surgeon, Dr. Craig Philem. So did Kaylie. Worse, he recognized her.

"Kaylie, Kaylie, Kaylie," he admonished with mock censure, reaching out an arm toward her. "Don't you know that our Dr. Leland makes time with *all* the best-looking nurses?"

"None of whom will give Craig here the time of day," Leland said with a wink, one arm draped casually about Kaylie's shoulders.

"You wish," Philem smirked, as Kaylie, to Stephen's disgruntlement, laughed and reached out to slide her free arm around the young surgeon's waist so that the three of them stood linked.

Both shorter and thicker than Leland, with receding sandy brown hair, the orthopedist was, nevertheless, an attractive man. His eyes alone commanded attention, being a bright, intense blue. Stephen glumly supposed that some women might find those dimples adorable, too.

Kaylie said something clever and chummy, no doubt, but

Stephen tuned it out, wondering sourly if she was on hugging terms with every doctor in the hospital. Targeting the two physicians, he decided that it was past time to get down to business.

"If you two are through pawing my nurse, I'd like to get out of here."

"Great!" Philem exclaimed. "How does tomorrow morning sound?"

"Right now sounds better."

"Not happening, champ," Leland said, strolling forward and lifting his stethoscope from around his neck. "Maybe if this was the first or only broken bone we had to worry about… As it is, though, I have to agree with Dr. Philem." Waving Stephen into silence, he popped in the earpieces of his stethoscope and slipped the bell beneath Stephen's T-shirt. After several seconds, he motioned Stephen forward, shifted and listened to his back. "Lungs are clear," he finally announced.

Philem stepped up, lifted the bedcovers and checked the color of Stephen's toes. "How's your pain level?"

"Eh," Stephen said with an unconcerned shrug of one shoulder.

Philem chuckled and glanced at Kaylie. "These hockey players are tough cookies. But seriously, is the leg bothering you?"

"Only when I move it," Stephen said.

"It'll get worse as the nerve block wears off," Philem warned. "But we'll do our best to get on top of it and stay there. Isn't that so, Kaylie?"

"Yes, sir. I just have one concern," she said, smiling at Stephen. "He's been having nightmares."

"Kaylie!" Stephen snapped, appalled.

"That's why this happened," she went on, ignoring him. "He broke the leg again when he fell out of the bed." She shifted her gaze to Brooks, adding, "I suspect that's what led to his rib injuries the other night, too."

"Kaylie!" Stephen barked again.

"Is that right?" Leland asked him. Then, without waiting for an answer, he shook his head. "I should have picked up on that."

"Those are some pretty violent nightmares," Philem noted.

"What happened to my right to privacy?" Stephen demanded. To his surprise, Kaylie turned on him.

"What are you talking about? I haven't breached any confidentiality. These are your doctors. They need to know how the drugs are affecting you."

"The drugs?" Stephen echoed uncertainly.

"She's right," Leland agreed, consulting a PDA that he'd drawn from a pocket. He rattled off several familiar-sounding drug names. "In combination, any two of those can, in some cases, induce nightmares. In a small number of patients, one of them can even cause hallucinations." He drew a prescription pad from a pocket, produced an ink pen and began to scribble. "Let's change the anti-inflammatory and the oral analgesic." After a few moments, he tore off the top sheet and handed it to Kaylie. "You can adjust the injections, too. May take a little tweaking, but I trust you to keep him comfortable without producing side effects."

Kaylie slid the prescription into her own pocket and nodded at Stephen. "I'll take care of him."

"Lucky stiff," Philem cracked. He launched into a series of instructions that Kaylie probably didn't need to hear and Stephen ignored.

Instead, he watched her, the classical lines of her profile drawing him like a lodestone. He understood now what she'd meant yesterday when she had mentioned "taking care of" his nightmares. He understood, too, that she had become indispensable to his well-being. When he'd said earlier that he needed her, he hadn't been exaggerating. Maybe he had been trying to schmooze her a bit, but the truth was that he didn't see how he could do this without her now.

Truth be told, Philem was right. He was lucky to have found her, and every instinct he possessed dictated that he hold on to her, which was why he didn't like watching these two white-coated mashers drool over her. Not that he was jealous or anything. It was just that, well, she was *his* nurse. That meant she was with *him*. Right? He was determined to make that clear to her at the first opportunity.

Her thoughtfulness and kindness touched and soothed him, and selfish as it might be, that was not something he meant to forego. She didn't need to know that his nightmares were all too real, though, so real that no drug in the world could possibly make a difference.

Predictably, Stephen's mood had soured again. Kaylie felt his disappointment at this new setback and sensed his need to be up and moving around. When she suggested that he take a ride in a wheelchair just to get out of the room, however, his horror was almost laughably palpable.

"I'm not getting into any wheelchair!"

"Oh, I do fear that you are," she said calmly. "How do you expect to get around otherwise?"

He glowered. "The same way as before."

She shook her head. "You can't put an ounce of weight on that leg until you get the walking cast, and I think you'll find that the length of this one changes your center of gravity so that even hopping around on one leg will be very difficult. Trust me on this. You aren't going farther than a few feet unless it's in a chair."

Stephen rolled his eyes. "Great. That's just great."

"It won't be forever," she pointed out, but he heaved a sigh and looked away.

Searching for some way to lighten his mood again, she made small talk and scrolled through the channels on the TV, none of which elicited more than a grunt of disdain from him. Then inspiration struck. She walked over to the bedside table and picked up the receiver of the telephone there. After checking the note in her pocket, she punched in a number and waited for the call to be picked up on the other end. A male voice answered almost immediately.

"Carter."

"Hello, Carter. It's Kaylie Chatam. Just thought I'd let you know that today would be a good time to stop by."

"Great! We've finished our shift, but I think the guys are all still around. I'll get them together, and we'll head over to the hospital. What's the room number?"

"Three-thirty."

"Give us fifteen minutes."

"Looking forward to it," she told him. Aware of Stephen's glower, she hung up, cocking an eyebrow at him in silent question.

"So now you're arranging dates on my time?" he demanded.

"What?"

"It's not enough that my doctors fall all over you? Now you've got to set up meetings with your other boyfriends when you should be taking care of *me?*" He stabbed a finger downward.

Kaylie gaped at him. Was he jealous? She laughed in answer to her own silly question. Jealous? Of little old her? No. The man was spoiled. He wanted her there to wait on him hand and foot. That was all. She parked her hands at her waist.

"You don't know what you're talking about."

"Don't I?" He tossed out a hand. "I'm not blind. I saw with my own eyes how they greeted you. Leland especially seems to think he has some claim on you. Isn't he a little too old for you?"

She couldn't help rolling her eyes. "Brooks Leland is my older brother Morgan's best friend, if you must know. He's like a member of the family, another brother almost."

"Oh." Stephen pondered that for a minute, his frown easing, but then the frown deepened again. "What about Philem? And don't tell me he's like a member of the family because I saw the way he looked at you."

Kaylie felt heat blossom in her cheeks. "We're friends."

"Baloney. There's something going on between you and Philem."

"We're not dating, if that's what you're implying."

Stephen's eyes narrowed thoughtfully. "But he's asked, hasn't he?" Suddenly, he grinned. "He asked, and you shot him down. Ha!"

"I didn't 'shoot him down,'" she insisted. "My father was very ill," she added defensively, "and I didn't feel I could be away from him."

Stephen's grin grew. "It's because Philem's going bald, isn't it?"

"It is not! I told you—"

"Yeah, yeah, Daddy was too sick at the time. And what's your excuse now?"

Kaylie blanched. "And now, we're friends," she told Stephen firmly, "*not* that it's any of your business."

The truth was that she and Philem had dated for a while, and she had liked him very well—still did like him—but when he'd kissed her, she'd suddenly found herself wanting to run in the opposite direction. After her father's heart attack, she'd used his physical condition to allow the relationship to wane. They had remained on friendly terms, but that's as far as it had gone. And as far as she would allow it to go.

"It is my business if you're making dates for three-thirty in the afternoon when you should be working for me!" Stephen insisted.

Kaylie went to the door and pulled it open. Pressing it all the way back, she stood against it, her arms folded, while he glowered in confusion. Finally, she pointed to the two-inches-high gold letters affixed to the door. Three-three-zero.

Stephen's eyes nearly popped out of his head, but then he recovered enough to accuse, "You gave my room number to someone." She nodded, a tad smugly perhaps. "Who?" Stephen demanded.

For once, Kaylie decided to get back a bit of her own. "Guess you'll find out when they get here." With that, she spun and left the room, the door smoothly swinging closed behind her.

"Kaylie!" Stephen yelled, but the door muffled the sound.

Ignoring him, she stepped far enough away that she couldn't hear. The nerve of the man, jumping to such conclusions, acting as if he owned her! Far worse was the unmistakable thrill that she felt because of it.

Dismayed, she reached out to the Lord of her life.

Father God, why him? Why couldn't Craig Philem make her heart trip? Or Brooks, even! Anyone else, anyone who could fit into her world. Anyone who shared her beliefs and lifestyle. Anyone her father might approve of. *Lord, I don't understand myself. Surely I'm just feeling sorry for him. Help me put these feelings into perspective. In the name of Jesus, help me.*

Linda Shocklea walked by with another nurse, took one look at Kaylie's face and stopped, nodding at her workmate, who went on her way. "The bear bit you, did he?"

Kaylie sighed. "Let's just say that I'm giving my patience a breather."

Linda chuckled. "It's a pity, isn't it, that such a good-looking guy is such a grouch?"

"Well," Kaylie said, feeling unaccountably protective of him, "he's been through a lot, and he still has a lot to get through."

"Mmm." Linda cut a knowing gaze in Kaylie's direction. "Honey," she drawled, "a man that handsome, if he was all healed up, I might let him bite me, too." She grinned and sauntered off, leaving Kaylie alternately gaping and sputtering laughter.

A moment later a male voice softly called her name, prompting Kaylie to turn in the opposite direction. A quartet of male smiles greeted her. As the four drew near, one of them asked, "How's he doing?"

"See for yourself," she said brightly, leading the way.

You gave my room number to someone. As if she would ever do anything to hurt him. She only hoped that she wasn't foolish enough to let herself get hurt.

"You may not remember these guys," Kaylie said as four young men crowded into the room. "They transported you to the hospital."

"I remember." Stephen acknowledged the paramedics with nods.

Having one leg in a cast made it difficult to kick one's self, but he would have dearly liked to do so. Barring that, he'd have been pleased for the floor to open up and swallow him whole, adjustable bed and all. As it was, he could only smile and shake hands all around. It was bad enough that he'd made a fool of himself over her and the doctors, but he should've known that she wouldn't give his room number to anyone who could or would harm him. To make matters worse, at least one of these fellows, Carter, was a real fan.

"Man, I saw your last shutout. Amazing game! One of the best I've ever seen."

Stephen gladly recapped that game with the guy. It kept

him from having to look at Kaylie. Eventually, he sent Carter to the drawer in the beside table where the autographed pucks were stored and saw them handed out.

"My agent's working on those game passes," Stephen told them. "I hope a game next season is okay. Playoff seats are just so hard to come by."

"Oh, hey, I'd rather see you play, anyway," Carter assured him. The others murmured agreement.

"Not that we'd turn down playoff tickets," one was quick to add.

Stephen chuckled. "I hear you. I'd sure rather be there than here myself."

Kaylie stepped in and put an end to the visit at that point. "Better let the patient get some rest, boys."

He did feel a little ragged, but when she glanced at her watch, he suddenly felt even worse. She was going to leave him here on his own again. It was nothing less than he deserved, of course, but he didn't like it. Still, he could not let her go without apologizing and at least trying to explain his behavior.

The paramedics dutifully filed out, waving and thanking him for the pucks.

"No, no," Stephen protested. "Y'all took good care of me. I appreciate it."

Carter was the last out the door. He smiled at Kaylie, waggled his puck at her and winked. Stephen felt a kick in his chest and an instant spike in his temper, and that's when it hit him that she was right, after all. He *was* jealous! Terribly so.

The knowledge took his breath away. For the first time in his life, he was actually jealous, and he didn't like it, not one little bit. The question was, what could he do about it? What should he do about it?

Helplessly, he watched her check her watch again, and the next thing he knew, he was pleading with her.

"Wait. Don't go yet. Just wait a minute, will you?" Well, that was another first: Stephen Gallow pleading with a woman. Usually, they threw themselves at him and he occasionally allowed himself to catch one. None of them had ever affected him as Kaylie did, though. "I—I have something to say."

Standing all the way across the room, Kaylie looked down at her toes, rocking back on her heels and folding her arms. He held his breath until she looked up again. Heart pounding, he held out his hand. She hesitated for a long moment, but finally she moved forward. Once she drew near, she put her hand in his. A ridiculous smile broke out on his face. It was insane, but he couldn't help a surge of nervous relief and sheer joy, especially when he gave her a tug and she came unresisting to the side of his bed. Looking down at her much smaller hand in his, he swept his fingers across her knuckles and spoke with blunt honesty.

"I've been unreasonable at times, even unbearable, and I apologize."

"No apology necessary," she told him softly, all forgiveness and generosity.

"I know that it's selfish of me to want to keep you to myself," he went on, squeezing her hand, "but it's so much easier when you're here."

"I understand," she said.

He shook his head. "I don't think you do. I'm not sure I understand it myself. When you're with me, I feel so…comforted, peaceful…hopeful, even, but it's more than that. It's…"

"It's what?" she asked, tilting her head.

He looked up into the purity of her face, her deep, dark, open gaze filling him with warmth. Her kindness and sweetness and patience enveloped him. A fierce yearning shook him to his core. Instinctively, he reached up, and then he was pulling her down, his hand clamped around the nape of her neck beneath the heavy weight of that crazy, looping bun that he hated simply because it kept her hair contained. She didn't have far to go. He surely stood more than a foot taller than she did, but he was partially sitting in a high bed, and she was already bending close. It seemed like an eternity, but no more than a heartbeat passed before their lips met.

What happened next could not be explained.

The room and everything else seemed to spin away. Sensation electrified every nerve ending in his battered body. At the same time, Stephen's mind clarified. He saw the stark reality of his own life.

He had been living, existing, in a kind of desert—a dry, cold, barren, lonely place where he didn't want to be anymore—and Kaylie was his first, perhaps his only, chance to escape it. She was warmth and shelter, companionship, contentment, peace—and much too good for the likes of him. She obviously knew it, too, for she suddenly wrenched away and fled the room.

Stephen collapsed back against his pillow, closed his eyes and prayed that he hadn't totally blown it. He suddenly did not see how he could do this, how he could put himself back together again and overcome this latest fiasco without her. He wasn't even sure that he wanted to try.

As the morning passed into afternoon and then into an interminable evening, he began to fear that he might not have a choice. His kiss might well have driven her away for good.

Chapter Eight

"Stupid, stupid, stupid," Kaylie murmured, pacing the hospital hallway the next morning. She still could not believe what had happened, what she had allowed to happen, the day before. That kiss had made her positively giddy—until she'd realized the implications.

She was not the sort of female that Stephen Gallow seemed accustomed to, and she certainly did not kiss her patients. What he must think of her now! She hadn't been able to face him after that kiss, and so she'd run. She'd stayed away because he was the last man with whom she ought to be getting involved. Her father, and very likely even her brothers, would disapprove. Why, *she* disapproved! She'd always assumed she'd find some quiet, bookish fellow with a clear calling to service, something they could share and work at together. Stephen Gallow was so far the opposite of her imagined mate that she couldn't think why she felt so drawn to him. But drawn to him she was, and so she'd cowardly stayed away.

That had been possible yesterday. The man was in the hospital, after all. Today he was supposed to go home to Chatam House, and that changed everything. Still, Kaylie had prayed long and hard before she'd decided to come here this morning. The inescapable facts were that, no matter how foolishly she had behaved yesterday, she was still a nurse, and he was still her patient. She had an obligation to Stephen Gallow.

Now that she was here, though, she couldn't bring herself to go into his room—not alone anyway. Thankfully, Craig Philem breezed into the corridor right on schedule.

"Good morning, Kaylie. Ready to take your guy home?"

Her guy. Gulping, Kaylie nodded and waved toward the door, inviting the doctor to go in. Ever the gentleman, however, Craig reached around her and pushed the door open, standing back so she could enter first.

"Kaylie!" Stephen exclaimed, his voice imbued with relief and concern.

Guilt stabbed her. He had been worried about her. She hadn't expected that. In fact, she'd assumed that he would be angry and petulant. For some reason, she'd rather have faced his anger than his concern. Fearing that he would immediately begin apologizing, explaining or cajoling in front of Craig, she sent him an imploring look, but he didn't even notice. He was too busy frowning at the doctor.

Craig, thankfully, did not seem to realize that anything might be amiss as he went about checking Stephen's vital signs. As he did so, Stephen sat quietly in the bed, his gaze on Kaylie. He seemed sad. Alarmed, she wondered if anything had gone wrong during the night.

"Heartbeat's a little rapid," Craig noted, stuffing his stethoscope back into his coat pocket. "You that anxious to get out of here?"

"More than anxious," Stephen said, looking directly at Kaylie. She couldn't quite manage to hold his gaze. Hers went skittering to Craig.

"How'd you rest last night?" Craig asked Stephen.

"Well enough, when they let me."

Craig chuckled. "Yeah, we slap you in here, tell you to rest, then we send the nurses in every couple of hours to hassle you. It's our way of keeping you from getting too comfortable."

"No worry on that score," Stephen muttered.

"You'll be glad to know, then, that I'm letting you go home."

"About time," Stephen said, closing his eyes and sighing.

Craig let them know that the nurse would be in shortly with discharge papers and written care instructions. "Not that you need them with Kaylie on the job. Strictly protocol."

Kaylie smiled and nodded in acknowledgment of the compliment.

"I've been told to ask you, though," Craig said to Kaylie, "when you might return to pediatrics." He slid his hands into his coat pockets. "Seems I'm not the only one missing you around here."

"Oh, I, uh, really couldn't say," she stammered. "Dad still depends on me."

"I thought your father's condition was stable."

"Well, yes, but his age and…" She waved a hand ineffectually.

Craig glanced at Stephen, nodding. "Mmm. I see. Other responsibilities."

She didn't know how to respond to that. On one hand, he seemed to have made a completely erroneous assumption. On the other, he was entirely correct. Suddenly she realized that he was about to leave her alone with Stephen.

Noting that Stephen's breakfast tray still rested on the rolling bed table, which had been pushed to one side, she rushed to snatch it up, saying, "I'll just get this out of the way."

Craig looked at the tray. It had barely been touched. Doctor and nurse spoke at the same time.

"Not eating much."

"You didn't drink your coffee."

Stephen shrugged. "Never found runny eggs and raw bacon appetizing. And that's not coffee. I think someone accidentally drained their crankcase into my cup."

"I'm sure Hilda will have something more appetizing for you," Kaylie told him. "Meanwhile, I'll run downstairs and get you a decent cup of coffee." That would keep her busy until the discharge nurse joined them.

Stephen shrugged listlessly again. Newly concerned, Kaylie followed Craig from the room, deposited the tray on the wheeled rack in the hallway and fled downstairs to the cafeteria, where she bought two tall coffees from a specialty vendor, her own disguised with French vanilla flavoring, sweetener and a goodly dose of cream. As shields went, it wouldn't provide much protection, but she cravenly prayed for distraction, at least, anything to prevent a repeat of yesterday's lunacy.

To her profound relief and surprise, Aaron Doolin was in the room, along with the nurse, when she returned. Apparently, Stephen had already made his own arrangements for transportation. Kaylie did not mention that they could have called on Chester. He would gladly have brought the aunties' town car for Stephen's use.

Stephen accepted the fresh coffee with placid pleasure and set about downing it as activity swirled around him. Kaylie's own concoction went barely tasted as things moved apace. She listened patiently to the nurse's discharge instructions, and then Aaron informed her that he called her aunts to let them know to expect Stephen shortly. As Stephen's legal rep, Aaron signed the papers then helped Stephen dress in loose burgundy sweatpants and a yellow-gold jersey from which Aaron's wife, Dora, had cut one of the sleeves. Kaylie slipped clean white socks onto Stephen's feet, marveling again at their size.

Just under an hour later, a nurse wheeled Stephen out to Aaron's waiting car. Kaylie was stunned to find out that Stephen had instructed Aaron to purchase a wheelchair for his use. That chair was already tucked into the trunk of Aaron's luxury sedan.

Kaylie saw Stephen settled onto the backseat of Aaron's car, then followed behind it in her own vehicle. When their little caravan arrived at Chatam House, they found Chester at the side entrance beneath the porte cochere, putting the finishing touches on the old wheelchair ramp that Grandpa Hub had used. Chester had pulled it out of storage and bolted it into place at Aunt Hypatia's instruction.

The ramp covered the redbrick walkway and steps and extended out onto the drive, forming a small, flat base where the chair could be positioned atop the deep gravel. The wood-and-metal structure needed a fresh coat of white paint, but that did not distract from the colorful beauty of the flowers that frothed beneath its railings and tumbled in brilliant disarray from the enormous terra-cotta pots flanking the bright yellow door with its austere black framing. Spiraling green topiaries stood sentinel next to the mounds of shrubbery that softened the stark, white-painted, quarried stone from which the great house was built.

As Kaylie waited for Aaron and Chester to take the wheelchair from the trunk of the car, she felt the full glory of spring surround her. Air as soft as cotton, sunshine as clear and bright as crystal and temperatures hovering in the seventies combined to sooth the soul. Brilliant green carpeted the expansive lawns of Chatam House, delighting the eye. Kaylie could even see a few small, creamy white blossoms peeking out from the waxy, dark green leaves of the enormous magnolia tree on the west lawn. She wondered if Aunt Mag's roses were blooming in the arbor on the east side of the house and couldn't believe that she hadn't even thought to check as she'd come up the drive earlier. Her thoughts then had been consumed with problems. Yet, here was proof of God's omniscience and care.

She stood aside and bowed her head, silently praying as Chester and Aaron eased Stephen out of the sedan and got him into the chair.

Forgive me, Father, for wallowing in my own angst. I know that You are with me every moment and that You will show me what to do and what to say if only I am brave enough to pay attention and obey. Help me, then, to help Stephen and, above all, to open his eyes to You. Amen.

She looked up straight into those solemn gray eyes, but Stephen quickly looked away. He had been unusually quiet all morning. In fact, an air of gloom hung over him. He sat silently while Chester attached a support sling to the chair for his broken leg. Troubled, Kaylie lightly touched Stephen's broad shoulder.

"Are you feeling okay?"

He glanced up, nodded and looked down again. Apprehension shivered through her. She did then what any nurse might have done; she laid her wrist against his forehead to check for a temperature. He jerked back as if she'd burned him. Feeling a tad scorched herself, despite discerning no telltale fever, she tucked her hands behind her.

A moment later, Chester maneuvered the chair around and pushed it up the ramp, remarking how he'd used to do this for old mister Hub senior. Aaron joked that the old fellow probably hadn't compared size-wise with a polar bear, implying that Stephen did. Stephen's lack of retort seemed to worry Aaron, who looked askance at Kaylie as he stood aside to allow her to enter the house ahead of him. She could do nothing more than wordlessly share his concern.

The darkness of the back hall embraced them, redolent with the aromas of old wood, beeswax, brick, tea and, unless Kaylie missed her guess, Hilda's fabulous gingerbread muffins. The old house seemed to take them into its arms, as comforting as one of the aunties' hugs. As they moved between the vast kitchen, butler's pantry, formal dining room and back parlor, Kaylie thought, as she often did, of the generations of Chatams who had called this house home over the past century and a half. In addition, this place had provided temporary sanctuary for countless other individuals, Stephen being just the latest.

Why, her cousin Reeves Leland and his adorable moppet Gilli had spent weeks and weeks here this past winter after discovering that honeybees had invaded the attic of their own place. Reeves had recently married Anna Miranda Burdett. They lived at Burdett House now, a lovely old Victorian just a few blocks away.

The aunties had hosted their wedding reception in the ballroom, and it had been a lovely, poignant, yet somehow light-hearted, affair that had made Kaylie wonder if she would ever know such joy. Conversely, after Reeves's wedding, her father had become adamant about her being called to remain single. Kaylie had struggled with the idea all along, but never more so than lately. She didn't even want to think why that might be.

Their group reached the end of the corridor and turned into the west hall, one of a pair that flanked the massive central staircase, which terminated in the south-facing foyer. Chester wheeled Stephen past the ladies' "withdrawing room"—the gents' opened onto the east hall between the library and the ballroom—and one of Kaylie's favorite chambers in the old house, the cloakroom. Though now a storage facility for galoshes, umbrellas and overcoats, Kaylie imagined it filled with everything from fur-lined capes, swirling great coats and top hats to fringed leather suede, ankle-length dusters and cowboy hats. The cloakroom had probably seen them all at one time or another.

Kaylie was not surprised when Chester turned Stephen's chair into the front parlor. She saw at once that the aunties had subtly shifted the furnishings to make way for the wheelchair. The sling supporting Stephen's right leg straight out in front of him complicated matters, however, and it took some maneuvering to bring him near the tea tray, especially with all three of the aunties directing traffic. Finally, things were arranged to their mutual satisfaction.

"Thanks," Stephen murmured to Chester, who nodded and went out.

Hypatia reclaimed her usual wingback chair and directed Aaron to its twin, while Magnolia sank down on one end of the settee and Kaylie assumed a seat next to Stephen on an English mahogany side chair brought forward for the occasion. Odelia, however, continued to hover over Stephen, waving her lacy handkerchief and fluttering the bell-shaped sleeves of the filmy white blouse that she wore with a brown fringed skirt, white moccasin-style loafers and clusters of turquoise beads that dangled almost to her shoulders.

"Welcome home! Welcome home, Stephen dear. You poor darlin'." In her enthusiasm, she bent and embraced him, her hands cupping his head, her earrings swinging in his face.

He shot Kaylie an amused glance that eased a small measure of her concern. "Thank you, ma'am."

"How you've suffered!" Odelia clucked. "We're so happy to have you back again." She patted his good hand. "Don't you worry a bit. We're going to get you well, no matter how long it takes. Isn't that so, Kaylie dear?"

Kaylie didn't even have time for a limp nod before Hypatia said, "For pity's sake, Odelia, sit down." Her tone could not be construed as anything but an order.

Unperturbed, Odelia trotted over and dropped down beside Magnolia, her sweet smile in place. Hypatia then turned to Stephen, offering him a more formal welcome.

"It is good to see you again, Stephen dear. May we offer you a refreshment?" She leaned forward, reaching for the teapot. "Cream or sugar?"

"Uh…" Stephen shook his head. Taking his response as a repudiation of the condiments, not the tea, Hypatia began to pour. Meanwhile, Ophelia popped up and piled a trio of dark, fragrant muffins on a delicate Limoges china plate, along with a slice of cantaloupe and a delicate silver fork. She handed him that plate just as Hypatia passed him a cup of black tea on a matching saucer. Stephen tried to accept both, but the muffin plate wound up in his lap.

Kaylie lurched forward and caught the plate and the muffins. The fork and cantaloupe hit the floor. Aaron laughed, but Ophelia went into paroxysms of apologies and reassurances.

"Oh! Oh, oh, oh! How clumsy of me! Your fruit!" She grabbed a heavy linen napkin, hiked her skirt and gave every evidence of intending to drop to her knees. Kaylie managed to head her off.

"Here, let me." Placing the muffin plate on the seat of her chair, Kaylie took the napkin from Odelia, bent and swept up both fork and cantaloupe slice, setting them aside on the tray.

"Kaylie to the rescue," Aaron chortled. "Getting to be a habit, huh, Stevie?"

Stephen winced but made no reply.

Magnolia shoved a plate of muffins, sans fork and fruit, into Aaron's hands as Hypatia reached once more for the teapot, asking in a strained voice, "Cream or sugar?"

Oblivious to any awkwardness, Aaron took both. Hypatia managed to prepare his tea while shooting daggered glances at Odelia, who returned meekly to her place on the settee.

Magnolia tsked and helped herself to a plate of goodies while Auntie Od bounced numerous regretful looks around the room. Kaylie selected another slice of melon for Stephen, spearing it with a clean fork. She placed it on his plate that way and returned the plate to his lap, within easy reach. She then filled another plate and passed it to Odelia with a sympathetic smile.

Subsiding back into her chair, Kaylie took Stephen's saucer from him, allowing him to use his good hand to handle his tea. He gave her a slight nod in thanks but failed to meet her gaze as he raised the cup and sipped. A muscle quivered in the corner of his eye, but his face remained expressionless, even as Aaron exclaimed, with a full mouth, over the muffins and slurped his tea. The muffins, Kaylie knew, were delicious, so she offered Stephen the saucer. He placed his teacup on it, and she set both aside as he reached down to take a muffin from the plate on his lap.

"Kaylie, dear, would you like a cup of tea?" Hypatia asked.

"Yes, thank you."

"And muffins?" Magnolia suggested, passing her a fresh napkin.

Considering that she only had two hands, Kaylie declined. "I'll share with Stephen."

Stephen smiled at her and bit off a hunk of a muffin. An instant later, bliss relaxed the muscles of his face and widened his eyes. "Mmm." He chewed and swallowed. "Wow. Even my *oma*'s gingerbread isn't this good."

Kaylie snatched one of the muffins from his plate as the aunties erupted into expressions of delight at Stephen's praise. The sugar-crisped crust protected the moist insides, rich with golden raisins and pecans. While Kaylie nibbled and Stephen gobbled, the Aunties explained in minute, and often conflicting, detail how Hilda prepared the luscious treat.

The subject quickly exhausted itself, at which point Odelia smiled at Stephen and said, "Perhaps Oma would like Hilda's recipe."

"She might," Stephen replied with a tired smile.

"And who is Oma, dear?" Magnolia asked. "Your cook?"

"My grandmother. *Oma* is Dutch for grandmother."

"How lovely!" Odelia exclaimed. "What's the Dutch word for aunt?"

"Tante."

"Tante. I like that. *Tante* Odelia."

Stephen polished off his second muffin and went to work on the melon, holding the slice suspended on the fork. He put it down without finishing it, and Kaylie noted the signs of fatigue in the droop of his shoulders and eyelids.

She interrupted a chummy discussion between Aaron and the Aunties to say, "I think Stephen should get upstairs now."

That presented a problem that Kaylie had mulled over off and on for the past two days. Grandpa Hub had depended on Chester to carry him up and down the stairs, but Chester had been a decade younger then, and at ninety-two Grandpa had been little more than skin and bones. Aaron honed in on the issue at once.

"Hey, next time I'll bring along some of your teammates," he joked to Stephen. Looking at the aunties, he explained, "The Blades have a couple of Swedes and a Russian who make Stephen look like their baby brother."

"Maybe Chester and Mr. Doolin can get Stephen up the stairs by turning the chair backward," Odelia suggested.

Kaylie didn't see how that would be possible, given the fact that Stephen's leg stuck straight out and blocked access to the front of the chair so no one could lift from that side. She doubted that anyone could lift Stephen up so many stairs, anyway. Nevertheless, they would likely need Chester's assistance. Magnolia went to get him while Kaylie maneuvered

Stephen's chair to the foot of the stairs. They both looked up that broad, gracefully curving staircase and knew that he was getting up there only one way.

"Do you think you can do it?" she asked him quietly as the aunts and Aaron arrived to offer support.

He snorted. "Do I have a choice?"

"We'll take it slow, rest along the way."

He nodded grimly. Chester arrived, and without any further discussion Stephen pushed up to his feet, or rather, foot.

"You sure about this?" Aaron asked, realizing what Stephen was about to do. "Maybe we could rig some sort of ramp." It would take a team of oxen to pull Stephen up such a steep slope, and everyone knew it.

"Just get over here and give me a hand," Stephen ordered.

Aaron pushed past Kaylie and slipped his shoulder under Stephen's good arm. The aunts worried aloud, but Chester merely remarked that he would take up the chair. Hoisting the contraption, he began to climb the stairs with it. Behind him, Stephen hopped up onto the bottom step, his bad leg held out at an awkward angle. Kaylie rushed to lend what aid she could.

It was a grueling, lengthy process that brought Kaylie to tears and both Stephen and Aaron to the brink of exhaustion. By the time Stephen dropped down into the chair again, he was moaning, Aaron's chest pumped like a bellows, and Kaylie had to surreptitiously wipe her eyes. She quickly wheeled the chair along the landing, through the sitting room of Stephen's suite and into his bedroom, where she, Aaron and Chester got him into bed.

While Chester went back downstairs and Aaron sagged against the bedpost, Kaylie quickly administered an injection of painkiller.

"And I thought I was tough," Stephen murmured, his eyelids sagging.

"You are unbelievably tough," she told him softly. "I don't know another man who could have managed that, not even my brother Chandler."

His light gray eyes opened, delving deeply into hers, and he whispered, "I was afraid you wouldn't come back."

"Of course I came back."

His eyelids drifted down again, and he breathed the words, "I need you to come back."

"I did," she said. "I will." She realized then just how true that was. "I'll come back for as long as you need me."

How, she wondered, as Stephen's hand sought and gripped hers, could she do anything else? She supposed it meant that they would have to discuss that kiss, but oh, how she wished they could pretend that it had never happened.

Aaron's cell phone rang just then, and he dug it from his jacket pocket, looked at the caller ID and winced before showing it to Stephen, who moaned low in his throat.

Kaylie glimpsed the photo of a mature, smiling woman with a long face and straight, shoulder-length, pale blond hair just before Aaron put the phone to his ear and exclaimed, "Hannah! How is *mijn favoriete meisje?*"

Even Kaylie knew that his accent was deplorable, though she had no idea what the phrase even meant. That it was Dutch, however, she did not doubt.

"Yeah, well, there have been a few developments," Aaron said reluctantly, glancing at Stephen. "Fact is, we just got our boy back here to the mansion from another little hospital stay." He emphasized the word *mansion.*

He listened for several moments before saying, "Uh, right, right! Thing is, I guess we were just too busy to think of it, little issue with his leg." Then, "Naw, naw, it's gonna be fine. Surgery was a complete success."

He glared at Stephen and pointed at the phone, but Stephen

shook his head adamantly, turned away and closed his eyes. Aaron bowed his head, balancing his forehead against the palm of his free hand, his arm wrapped around the bedpost. "Yeeaah," he drawled, "the thing is, see, he's asleep. His nurse gave him a shot, and he went out like a light, let me tell you." He straightened, looked at Kaylie and pointed to the small phone nestled against his ear, as if to ask that she confirm his assertion.

Kaylie spread her hands, glanced at Stephen and shook her head, silently indicating her confusion and reluctance to get involved.

Aaron smoothly shifted gears, his jocular mien sliding over him like a second skin. "Hey, you ought to see this place. It's really something, an honest-to-goodness antebellum mansion. They've got a dumbwaiter out on the landing, murals on the ceilings and enough crystal hanging around to bury a fellow if it should fall. Why, your boy's resting on rare antiques, or so I'm told."

He suddenly stood upright, eyes wide. "Uh, uh, let's wait on that a few more days." Turning to Kaylie, he churned his hand, silently asking her for help, but what help? "U-until the, um, doctors o-okay him for visitors." Grimacing, he showed his teeth to Kaylie. "No, really. It's j-just a precaution. Yeah, yeah, of course I'll tell him you called." Aaron laughed in that practiced way of his and went on. "Now, don't worry about him. He's in good hands, and I'm sure he'll be well enough to speak to you in, uh, soon."

After a few more seconds, Aaron ended the call and slumped against the bedpost once more. "Whew! Thought for a minute there that she was about to jump a plane."

"She'd better not!" Stephen growled, flopping onto his back.

Kaylie parked her hands at her hips and demanded, "What is going on? Who was that?"

Stephen clamped his mouth in a hard line, but Aaron

seemed surprised that Kaylie didn't know. "Hannah Scherren, Stevie's mom."

"His mother!" Kaylie bent toward the bed. "You don't want your mother here? Why ever not?"

Stephen rubbed a hand over his face. "I just don't, that's all."

"But she's your *mother.*"

"Listen," Aaron said suddenly, "I gotta run." He started off, then paused and turned back to shake a finger at Stephen. "The thing is, if you would just talk to her, it might do you both a world of good."

"Stay out of it, Aaron."

Aaron sighed. "Been four years since you last spoke to any member of your family, Stevie."

"I said to stay out of it!"

"Not since the funeral."

Kaylie gasped. "What funeral? Whose? What are you talking about?"

Aaron shook his head and made for the door again. "You want to know that, you gotta ask Steve."

Kaylie turned back to the bed, but Stephen's glare warned her not to press the issue. "Don't," he said when she opened her mouth.

Curiosity and concern burned within her, but she knew that it would be a mistake to become further involved with Stephen Gallow's personal life. She closed her mouth and sat down in the wheelchair next to the bed. Stephen closed his eyes, and after a moment, his hand groped for hers. Kaylie did her best not to reach out, but somehow their palms met, and their fingers intertwined. She sat with her head bowed, asking herself what she was doing with this man, until the pressure of his fingers slowly eased. Finally, she slipped free and left him sleeping peacefully.

Moving out into the sitting room, she lifted a hand to the

back of her neck and then turned her eyes heavenward. The mystery of Stephen Gallow had just deepened, and the differences between them had never been more painfully obvious, and yet…and yet…

"Show me Your purpose in this, I beg You."

A man who would not even speak to his own mother could not be for her.

But could she be for him?

Chapter Nine

*A*lone again.

That was Stephen's first thought when he woke. Alone and in pain, considerable pain, more than he'd expected, but nothing he couldn't manage until Kaylie came again.

I'll come back for as long as you need me.

He had carried her whispered promise off into exhausted, thankfully peaceful slumber, but he couldn't forget now how appalled she had been that he wouldn't speak to his mother. How could he tell her why? She would likely despise him then, as his family must.

I'll come back for as long as you need me.

Yet, she'd thought that he hadn't needed her in the hospital, and she had stayed away. Now she had to know that there was much wrong in him. Would she break her promise? Or would she simply go away for good?

The sound of her voice came to him, growing louder as she crossed the sitting room toward his bedchamber.

"I'm sorry, Dad. I know I've been gone more than usual today, but this is a special case."

Pleased and surprised, Stephen opened his eyes and strained to hear every word.

"You know that he just got out of the hospital."

Pushing up onto his elbow, Stephen looked into the sitting room, listening shamelessly, but Kaylie must have come to a stop just out of sight.

"I'm sorry you had to make your own lunch, but I came home as soon as I could to put a casserole in the Crock-Pot, didn't I?"

A pause followed, then, "I can't be sure when he'll wake up, but don't feel you have to wait to eat until I get there." And finally, "Okay, fine. I'll come as soon as I can. I promise. Bye."

Stephen eased back down on the bed, calling out, "Kaylie?"

Just as expected, she stepped into the doorway, her old flip phone in her hand, a smile on her face. "You're awake! You must be hungry. You slept straight through lunch."

"Did I?"

He licked his lips, aware now of his hunger and thirst. As if she could read his mind, she walked to the bedside table, pocketed her phone and poured him a glass of water, saying, "I brought this up fresh just a little while ago."

Turning onto his side, he took the glass in his good hand and managed a long drink before collapsing back onto his pillow. "Thanks."

"You're welcome. So how do you feel?"

"Like I've been beat up."

"The leg's starting to ache, isn't it?"

"How'd you know?"

"I'm surprised the nerve block hasn't worn off already," she said, smiling down at him. "Do you want something for pain before I go down to get your meal?"

He shook his head. "I don't want to go back to sleep. What time is it, anyway?"

"Nearly four."

He nodded, and she turned away, but he called her back. "Kaylie?"

"Yes?"

"Thank you for staying."

"I wasn't here all the time."

"I know, you went home to put on dinner for your dad, but you were here most of the time, weren't you?"

She looked down at her hands. "I thought you might need me."

"I do."

She said not a word to that; neither did she meet his gaze.

"Will you stay while I eat?" he asked tentatively.

She nodded. "Someone has to take down your tray when you're done."

"Thanks," he said, but then before she could get out of the room, his big mouth got the better of him and he halted her again. "Kaylie?"

She stopped and turned her head, gazing at him over her shoulder. "Yes?"

He was having second thoughts, but the idea had been uppermost on his mind since she'd walked into his hospital room that morning, and the sooner it was out, the sooner they could honestly address it. And the sooner he would know where she truly stood on the matter. Last night he'd thought she was done with him; then she'd walked into his room this morning. He tamped down his misgivings and said, "I hope you don't regret that kiss. Because I don't."

She froze for several heartbeats, but then she turned, her body pivoting at the end of her neck, and calmly asked, "Why won't you speak to your mother?"

He must have looked as if he'd been poleaxed, because that's how he felt. She flipped around and walked out of the room. He stared at the empty door for several long seconds, but then he had to smile, even as his stomach sank.

Oh, man. Talk about giving as good as she got! Her message couldn't have been more clear. If he tried to discuss the one subject, she would insist on discussing the other, and that was the last thing he wanted. The very last thing. Mercy, his gentle little nurse had just backed him into a corner and forced a standoff. These, he understood perfectly, were the conditions under which they would proceed: the kiss hadn't happened, no estrangement from his mother. He supposed he'd just have to live with that, whether he liked it or not.

She returned in less than twenty minutes with his lap desk and a dinner tray. Hilda had outdone herself with a dish that Kaylie called "drover's pie," consisting of tender bits of beef in a thick, dark gravy presented in a nest of mixed vegetables surrounded by a hearty helping of mashed potatoes and topped with a flaky biscuit crust. It beat by a mile the bland, anemic meal that the hospital had served him the night before. Add to that bounty a huge dish of banana pudding that was to die for, and Stephen wound up stuffing himself. Thoroughly sated, he leaned back against the stack of pillows behind him and sighed.

"I may just have to steal that woman away from your aunts when I leave here. Man, can she ever cook."

Kaylie chuckled. "If you want to see what damage three little old ladies on the warpath can do, you just try that."

He laughed. "Yeah, I can just image your aunts coming after me with hoes and pitchforks. Hypatia, of course, would be wearing pearls and pumps, and all the more terrifying for it, while Magnolia sported galoshes and heavy gardening gloves."

Kaylie snorted behind her hand. She had brought the desk chair in from the other room and sat with her legs crossed at the knee, watching him pack it in. Oddly, she'd seemed to derive some sort of pleasure from watching him eat. His mother had done that when he'd been a little boy. Kaylie, however, was not his mom, and he was no boy now.

"And Aunt Odelia?" she asked, a smile wiggling on her lips.

He considered and decided, "Viking gear, complete with finger bones dangling from her earlobes and a horned helmet."

"Except she'd tie bows on those horns," Kaylie said, giggling.

He laughed at the thought of it, but then he shivered. Odelia would probably use his intestines to tie those bows. Still, that Hilda was some cook. It might be worth the risk.

"I don't know how you could pass up that drover's pie," he mused. It was the wrong thing to say.

"I promised Dad I'd have dinner with him," Kaylie murmured. She checked her watch then hastily rose and took the tray from his lap desk. He was really starting to hate that watch of hers. "How's your pain level?"

"I'll live," he muttered, though the leg had started to throb pronouncedly.

"Let me send this down to the kitchen, then we'll address that."

She went out, supposedly to send the tray down to the kitchen via the dumbwaiter, and returned a few minutes later. Moving to the bedside table, she picked up several small prescription bottles there and began to go through them one by one.

"I had these filled earlier on my way back here." She went through them one by one. "Anti-inflammatory. You take it after you eat. Nutritional supplement. Aids in repairing the bone. Antibiotic, twice a day for the next four days. Just a precaution. Pain med. One shouldn't knock you out. Two might, but not likely. You'll definitely feel them, though. The new injection obviously puts you on your back, so we'll save that for bedtime and extreme instances." She uncapped and shook out pills from all four bottles, then dumped the pills into his palm and handed him the water glass from the bedside table. "Bottoms up."

He dutifully swallowed the collection of capsules and tablets and drained the glass.

"Now let's get you in and out of the bathroom before those hit you. Okay?"

"Yes, please."

She carried the desk chair back into the sitting room and pushed in the wheelchair, but it quickly became obvious that the positioning of his leg would make the chair useless in such close confines. He didn't mind. It meant that he'd have his arm around her while he hopped to and from the bath.

They went through the laborious process, him hopping on one foot, Kaylie steadying and supporting him. He was relieved to find that he could still do pretty well for himself once he actually got where he was going. His left leg was apt to be twice as strong as the right before this was over, though. He made a mental note to have Aaron speak to the team kinesiologist first thing tomorrow, then he had to stop and think what day this was. Thursday, he decided. Yes, definitely Thursday. The team was playing tonight.

By the time he got back to Kaylie, he was aching all over. Nevertheless, he insisted that she put him in the wheelchair and push him into the sitting room so he could watch the pregame show and the hockey game to follow. She did so reluctantly and only after explaining the functions of the chair and showing him how to operate it. Wasn't much to it. As it was all hand-operated and he had the use of only one hand, he wouldn't be going very far in the thing by himself, anyway.

She fetched his phone from his bedside table and gave it to him, along with a slip of paper that she pulled from a pocket. "This is the telephone number here at Chatam House. If you need anything, call the phone here and Chester will come up."

"But I can still call you, right?"

"Of course. It's just that Chester's closer and can take care of most of your needs. I'll be back later to give you your injection. Okay?"

"Okay, but that's hours from now."

"True. So, in the meantime, if you need anything call on Chester."

He shoved his hand through his hair. "Surely you see that I have greater need of you now than I did before this cast covered my whole leg. Besides, you have no idea how boring it is being stuck here with nothing to do and no one to talk to."

"Well, you have the TV," she said, plucking the remote from the mantel, "and there are books on the bedside table. Plus, you have your phone."

He rolled his eyes and snapped, "Fine. You weren't hired to keep me company. I get it."

"It's just that I have other responsibilities," she said a tad defensively, "and I've already been here more today than I expected because I had to be sure how the new meds would affect you."

"Whether they'd give me nightmares, you mean."

"Yes, among other things."

He had not, fortunately, dreamed at all—not that he remembered, anyway. In fact, now that he thought of it, the nightmare hadn't come since the doctors had changed his prescription. The lack of nightmares didn't change the reality, however.

He averted his gaze, shrugging. "Guess I'll see you later then."

"Yes. See you later."

She handed him the television remote and went out.

Loneliness swamped him the instant she left his sight.

Appalled, he shook his head. It wasn't that he was actually lonesome. Of course it wasn't! He'd been living alone for the better part of a decade now. Good grief, could he not be alone in a suite of rooms in a house full of people without becoming maudlin about it?

He toyed with the idea of calling Aaron and getting him down here to watch the game with him, but Aaron had already made that onerous drive once today, and Stephen really couldn't, in good conscience, ask him to make it again. He wondered whom else he might call and thought of his mother. Suddenly the need to hear the sound of her voice welled up in him, but the next instant Nick's face wavered before his mind's eye. Gulping, Stephen pushed away that vision, along with any desire to contact his mother. What other choice did he possibly have?

Ten minutes later, he was pecking out a text message to Kaylie, informing her that the game would be over by ten.

"It's ready, Dad," Kaylie said, setting the casserole dish on the cast-iron trivet in the center of the kitchen table next to a tossed green salad. "Will you bring the bread?"

"It's not right," Hub rasped, continuing with a theme that he'd been harping on since she'd gotten home. "You should be able to eat undisturbed at a decent hour."

It was forty minutes past their usual dinnertime, a mere forty minutes, and they tended to eat early, but Kaylie said nothing. It would help if Stephen would refrain from texting her every half hour or so. Still, she couldn't help thinking of the way Stephen had enjoyed Hilda's drover's pie tonight.

She smiled to herself, remembering the appreciative sounds he'd made and the expressions of bliss on his handsome face. It had been thoughtful of Hilda to cook a dish that he could eat with one hand and to have it ready early. Otherwise, they would have had to find something to tide him over until the aunties' normal dinner hour, which was about twenty minutes from now. Hilda had said she'd done it because Stephen had missed lunch, but Kaylie suspected that it was a combination of Hilda's compassion and Stephen's complimentary remarks regarding her gingerbread muffins. Kaylie's own cooking did not receive such high marks from her father.

"And we ought to be able to count on a decent dinner," Hub went on, carrying the loaf of whole wheat bread to the table from the kitchen counter by its plastic sleeve, "not these hastily thrown together, one-dish concoctions that are all you have time for now. Your mother would have laid a proper table and provided a balanced meal."

Kaylie let her exasperation show, placing one oven-mitted hand on her hip and gesturing toward the table with the other. "What is wrong," she asked, "with place mats, dinner plates, napkins, forks, knives, spoons and drinking glasses? Isn't that an adequate table setting? And where do you think I got the recipe for this casserole? From Mom, that's who! I'm sorry she's not around to serve it, but that's not my fault."

Hub reared back as if she'd struck out at him. "So, you think it's *my* fault?"

"Of course not!"

"Will you blame God then?"

"Never! It's no one's fault. Sometimes life just is what it is, and we have to deal with it as best we can."

"We were dealing very well, I thought, until you took this job," Hub grumbled, pulling out his chair.

"Were we?" Kaylie asked, divesting herself of the oven mitts. "Were we really dealing well?"

He set his jaw mulishly. "What's that supposed to mean?"

Kaylie sighed, pulled out her chair and sat down, choosing her words carefully. "Lately I've realized that we've been locked away inside this house for too long. We still have ministries to perform."

Hub took his seat, his mouth a thin, severe line. "I devoted my life to ministry."

"Dad, you speak as if your life is over!"

"That part of my life is, given my age and health."

"You could live another twenty or thirty years. Just look at Grandpa Hub. He was ninety-two when the Lord took him home and still overseeing his investments and charities from his wheelchair."

A look of such bleakness overcame her father that Kaylie wanted to weep. She reached for his hand. Though gnarled and pale, it still felt strong to her. Only his spirit, it seemed, was weak.

"You may be content to putter around your garden and sit in your chair for the next twenty years, Dad," Kaylie said softly. "You are certainly entitled to, but I am young and healthy, and the only thing I know without any doubt about myself right now is that I am called to nursing."

"But are you called to nurse this particular man?" Hub asked, gripping her hand hard.

"Yes," she answered without hesitation, a little shocked that she did not have to mull that over first, especially considering her mixed feelings and many hours of prayer on the matter.

Hub released her. "I am not so sure. You're alone with him too much. He's too young and pushy. We know nothing about him. He—"

"He's gravely injured and cannot manage on his own," Kaylie interrupted, folding her hands in her lap and bowing her head. "Will you pray over our food or shall I?"

Hub cleared his throat, and Kaylie prepared herself for a long, sermonizing monologue of the sort to which Hub had only rarely resorted during his career as a preacher. Instead, he quickly asked for a blessing on the food and left it there. Grateful for that, Kaylie tried to be as pleasant as possible throughout the meal and into the evening, though her mind never wandered far from Stephen and how he might be doing.

She felt terrible guilt for leaving Stephen there on his own—and terrible guilt at the idea of leaving her father to go and check on Stephen. Reminding herself that her father truly would be alone, whereas Stephen could call upon her aunts and the staff at Chatam House, she forced herself to remain at home. She had texted Stephen that he should call when he was ready for bed. When that happened, she would go to him.

But Stephen did not call, and it was not duty that finally drove her to make her excuses to her frowning father and rush over to Chatam House. She didn't know what it was exactly, but it felt horribly like longing, and so she whispered a prayer before she started the engine of her car.

"Lord, guide me. I am so confused, so torn. I'm not sure how to help either Stephen or Dad. I want Your will in all things, so I ask You please to reveal Your will to me in unmistakable ways. I know I should be able to discern and decide, but I don't trust myself to know what is best. I don't even know what *I* want!"

That brought her to a shocking halt, for it was a blatant lie. She did know what she wanted. She wanted to fulfill her calling as a nurse. She wanted to marry and have children. She wanted her father to find joy in this final stage of his life. She wanted to spend time with Stephen—not just see to his medical needs, but to spend time with him.

"But are those the right things to want?" she asked her Lord.

Dashing a tear from her eye, she laughed at her own confusion, opened her heart to God and just let it be for the moment.

Some ten minutes later Kaylie parked her convertible with the top up under the porte cochere at Chatam House and let herself in via the side door. Though not yet ten o'clock, the house was quiet. She walked the darkened hallways with an odd sense of anticipation, turned through the foyer and climbed the stairs without seeing another soul. As she moved along the landing toward the front of the house and Stephen's suite, her way was partially lit by the gray light of the television emanating from his open doorway. She was halfway there when he roared in apparent anguish.

"Aaarrrgh!"

She broke into a run, swinging through the door and into the sitting room, just in time to see Stephen pound his good right fist on the arm of his wheelchair.

"Forty seconds!" Stephen howled, glancing over his shoulder at her. "He lets them go ahead with forty seconds left to play!"

Kaylie slumped against the back of the sofa, one hand splayed over her heart and gasped, "You scared me."

"We were tied," Stephen barked at her, "and Kapimsky let them score!" He raised a hand and made a grasping motion at the television screen, as if he might pluck this Kapimsky off his skates. "Forty seconds from overtime."

Suddenly, his demeanor changed. Sitting forward, he lifted his fist at the TV. "Go, Smitty, go. Deke left, deke left. No! Left. Aw, man. Their goalie's a strong right, so he always expects a shot from the left. You fake left, then you shoot right." A buzzer sounded, and Stephen threw up his hand.

"I take it they lost," Kaylie said, starting around the sofa. Her heart still hammered. In those few seconds before she'd entered the suite, she'd imagined him on the floor in pain, having re-injured himself yet again, and the guilt had been heavy indeed. For whose fault would it have been except her own?

Stephen muted the television and curtly nodded for her to sit on the couch. "They lost," he confirmed, "in the last *forty seconds!* Unbelievable." He shook his head.

Kaylie gladly dropped down onto the cushions. "So is it over for them?"

He shook his head. "Naw, this is a seven-game series, but we're down two-to-one now." Sighing, he rubbed his forehead and shifted in his chair. "I should have been in the pipes tonight. I should be there for my team!" He smacked the arm of his chair with his palm, punctuating his words. "I deserve to be cut after this. Stupid. Stupid. Stupid."

"Well, yes, it is stupid for you to think like that," Kaylie said bluntly.

Stephen looked up in some surprise then shifted again, saying, "Look, I did this to myself, okay?"

"Okay. That doesn't mean you deserve to be cut from the team, especially for what happened tonight. That's on them." She swept a hand, indicating the casts on his arm and leg. "This is on you, and you've suffered mightily for it. Still are, judging by the way you keep fidgeting in that chair."

Stephen sighed and pointed the remote at the television. "I just want to hear the post-game—"

"Uh, no," Kaylie said, taking the remote from his hand.

What was it with the men in her life lately? One insisted that his life was essentially over, and the other seemed determined to beat himself up even more than he already had.

"You need rest and medication." She pointed the remote and shut off the television, tossing the small, rectangular black box onto the sofa, then moved behind his chair. The fact that he didn't argue confirmed her diagnosis.

"Watch the drinking glass," he mumbled.

"Hmm? Where?"

He reached down and came up with a tall crystal tumbler. "Your aunt was good enough to bring me a glass of apple juice earlier."

"Ah." Kaylie smiled to herself. She took the glass from him and carried it to the desk, where she left it, intending to take it downstairs with her later. "Odelia, I presume."

He held up a finger. "That's *Tante* Odelia."

Kaylie laughed, moving back to grasp the handles of his chair. "Can you get the brake?" He leaned forward and flipped the lever that freed the wheels. She rocked the wheelchair back and then shoved it forward. "So Odelia's styling herself as your *tante* now, is she?"

"Something like that."

"Look out," Kaylie teased, swinging the chair around in order to back through the door. "She'll be adopting you into the family if you're not careful."

"I wouldn't mind," he said after a moment, a wistful tone in his voice.

"I expect your mother would," Kaylie pointed out softly.

"I doubt it," he replied, shaking his head, "not after everything that's happened." He quickly changed the subject then. "My father certainly wouldn't. He washed his hands of me long ago."

Kaylie brought the chair to a halt beside the bed and set the brake with her foot. "I—I can't imagine such a thing."

He shot a wry look over one shoulder. "We're a pair, huh? Your father doesn't want to let go of you. Mine doesn't give me the time of day."

"H-how do you know that? About my father, I mean."

Stephen shrugged, not looking at her. "Little things you've said. A phone conversation I overheard. The fact that you still live at home."

"Not still," she said, knowing that she sounded defensive. She walked around to stoop and adjust the foot and leg rests so he could stand.

"Right. *Again,*" Stephen acknowledged dryly. "You're living at home *again*. And your father likes it that way."

"Is there anything wrong with that?" she asked, straightening and backing away.

"I don't know," Stephen said, putting his good foot on the floor. "Is there?" Pushing up with his good arm, he levered his weight onto his foot. Kaylie moved into position to assist him, using the need to do so to forestall answering his question. He didn't press it. Nevertheless, she felt compelled to answer him. He motioned toward the bathroom, and she helped him take two hopping steps in that direction. Grasping the door frame with his good hand, he prepared to move inside on his own, and Kaylie suddenly found herself blurting the truth.

"He thinks I shouldn't marry, just stay home and take care of him."

Stephen leaned against the door frame, twisting so that he could face her, one eyebrow cocked.

"Some are called to remain single," she defended, lifting her chin. "Just look at my aunts. None of them have ever married—though I've heard that Auntie Od and Mr. Copelinger down at the pharmacy might have if…" She shook her head over the irrelevancy of that. "It even says it in the Bible."

"You're kidding. I thought the Bible was all for marriage."

"Well, yes, except for certain circumstances, then it's better not to marry."

Stephen studied her for several seconds. Abruptly, he turned away, hopping through the door.

"Sweetheart," he said, shaking his head, "if ever I've met a woman meant to be a wife, it's you."

He hopped around to catch the edge of the door and push it closed, but her hand came up, seemingly of its own volition, and blocked it. Cocking an eyebrow, he waited.

"Wh-what makes you say that?" Somehow, she just had to know.

Stephen tilted his head and leaned down, bringing them nose to nose. She saw that he was trembling and feared that his strength had played out, but she waited breathlessly for his reply anyway.

"Because," he said, the very lightness of his voice heavy with meaning, "you're the first woman I've met that I would even consider marrying."

Chapter Ten

❧

Because you're the first woman I've met that I would even consider marrying.

The words echoed inside Kaylie's head. Stephen would consider marrying her. She was the first woman whom he would consider marrying. Consider. Marrying.

Suddenly she found herself reliving that kiss. She felt the connection again, the surprising excitement and rightness of it, the unfamiliar warmth and yearning. It was the last that had frightened her so, causing her to jerk back. Blinking, she was astonished to find that Stephen had pushed the door closed in her face.

She comprehended two facts simultaneously. One, several moments had passed. Two, she was in grave danger of losing her heart.

The hopelessness of the situation swamped her.

Her father was already convinced that she had been called to remain single, but even were he not, he would certainly never approve of her marrying a man like Stephen Gallow. Should she do so, she might well find herself more at odds with her father than her brother Chandler was, even estranged from him. Hub disapproved of Chandler's lifestyle, finding the sometimes hard-drinking, hard-partying, often brutally dangerous atmosphere of the pro rodeo circuit unsupportive of a Christian lifestyle, despite the Cowboy Church "phenomenon," as he called it. Would Hub think any better of hockey?

She couldn't imagine that he would, and she had always strived to honor her parents with her choices and decisions. How could she abandon that now, and was that not what a romantic involvement with Stephen would require? Suddenly she wanted to run for the hills again, to get as far away from this temptation as she could. Blindly, she started for the door, only to stumble into Stephen's wheelchair—and the realization that she could not leave him.

The man could barely get around with assistance; on his own, he was trapped. She was bound by duty, both as a nurse and a Christian, to help him. His physical condition was still serious, but his spiritual condition might well be even more acute. No, she could not abandon him, and if her duty to her father came into conflict, well, that was her problem alone. Stephen was weak and in pain and…lost.

As exasperating as her father could be, as sad as her mother's passing had been, Kaylie had never doubted that she was treasured by them. Thanks to them, she had grown up grounded in the surety of God's love for her and the absolute belief that nothing could ever separate her from such love, not time or space or even death. But what surety did Stephen have? She sensed genuine friendship between him and Aaron, but how certain could Stephen be about that when Aaron depended on Stephen for income?

It seemed to her that Stephen really had no one. And how unnecessary that was when Jesus stood waiting with open arms!

Lord, she prayed, *please let Stephen see You in me and my family. Let him turn to You and find the love that You bear for him. And please, Lord, teach my heart how to love Stephen as You would have me love him. To Your glory.*

The door opened behind her, and she turned to find Stephen sagging against the frame once more. He looked haggard and weary, his jaws unshaved and his pale eyes sunken. Her heart turned over. She quickly pushed the wheelchair out of the way and went to help him.

"Let's get you off your feet."

"Foot," he corrected with a crooked grin, his arm sliding across her shoulders.

"All the more reason," she said, mindful of his battered ribs and collarbone as she attempted to aid his progress.

At last, he sank down on the bed, and she briskly went about setting the covers to rights, something she should have done while he was in the bathroom. He smiled faintly as she tugged and tucked and smoothed, then dutifully swallowed his meds and submitted himself to an injection. As he settled onto his pillow again, his gray eyes sought hers.

"Will you stay with me for a while?"

"Of course," she said, after only the briefest hesitation.

Nodding toward the wheelchair, he said teasingly, "Your turn."

Laughing lightly, she pulled the chair close to the bed and sat. She waited for him to choose a topic of conversation, even as she feared what it might be. Instead, he reached down for her hand and closed his eyes. Sometime later, she realized that he had drifted off to sleep. Still, she stayed, her hand in his, until her own drowsiness drove her to her feet and at last sent her home.

Because you're the first woman I've met that I would even consider marrying.

The words floated into Stephen's consciousness, and for

that stupid remark, he silently called himself every derogatory name in the book: fool, idiot, lunatic, dimwit. When he ran out of English versions, he switched to Dutch: *dwass, krankzinning, stom,* even *hersenloos.*

How he could have been so brainless as to say such a thing he could not imagine. In truth, he had fully expected her to be gone when he'd hobbled out of the bathroom, to run as she had after that kiss, but she'd surprised him yet again. Not only had she been there, she'd smiled so benignly that his worst fears had evaporated and the treasured peace that she seemed to bring had settled around him.

He had allowed her gentle bullying and fussing, meekly swallowing her pills, suffering her injections and putting up with a tuck-in routine that a five-year-old would find insulting.

Oh, who was he kidding? He enjoyed every quiet order that came out of her mouth, every smile that curved her rosy lips, every delicate sweep and light pat of her fingertips. He reveled in them, truth be told. Such caring and tenderness had been absent from his life for far, far too long, so long that he hadn't even realized how much he had missed them until Kaylie Chatam had begun caring for him.

Relieved of every discomfort and disgustingly exhausted, he had craved sleep but he also craved connection with Kaylie. Intending to make conversation, he'd teased her into staying. When she'd willingly complied, he'd availed himself of her hand, marveling anew at its daintiness, but instead of conjuring conversation to keep her with him, his mind had turned to blankness. Now, once more, he would awake alone.

He didn't understand why that mattered so much all of a sudden. After Nick had died, Stephen had known that he was truly alone, forever separated from his family by loss and guilt. He had learned to live with it. Until now.

Now, he wanted to think that Kaylie cared for him, as

opposed to "took care of him." The difference was significant. The first implied an emotional connection; the second, a simple, professional one. He wanted that emotional connection badly, craved it with a desperation that frightened him.

For a moment, Stephen wondered if his concussion had addled his brain worse than the doctors had assumed. Since losing Nick, he had eschewed all but the most basic emotional connections for years, telling himself that was safer all the way around. Besides, he was too busy establishing his career. His game could not afford such distractions.

He had shut out everyone and everything not essential to his concentration on hockey and his performance on the ice. When he indulged in social occasions, it was most often at the behest of team management, in the interest of team morale or just to shut up Aaron. All work and no play, as the saying went. Even his "romantic" relationships had been brief, shallow and selfish on both ends.

He hadn't realized just how selfish he could be, though, until he'd taken Kaylie's hand in his last night and wished Kaylie's father would disappear so that Kaylie herself might not.

He opened his eyes, and to his everlasting surprise, Kaylie was there, sitting in a patch of bright sunshine that poured through the window next to the bed. Wearing lime-green scrubs, her hair in a ponytail, she sat quietly in his chair sorting pills into tiny cups arranged in a small plastic tray on her lap. He caught a pleased, energizing breath, and she looked up. Smiling, she quickly dispensed several more pills before speaking.

"Good morning. I was just organizing your meds for the next few days. How do you feel?"

His stomach growled as if in response, and she laughed, tucking the tray into the drawer of his bedside table. "We can take care of that."

Atop the table stood a tall, disposable cup of coffee in a foam rubber insulation sleeve. Rising from his chair, she removed the cup from its protective holder, clasping it between her palms.

"Not hot but warm enough, I think. Breakfast will be up in a few minutes. Meanwhile, you can work on this."

He used his elbow to dig his way higher in the bed while she took out a paper-covered straw, peeled it and slid it into the opening in the top of the coffee container.

"You're not just beautiful, you're a genius," he said as she passed him the cup. She ducked her head as he tentatively slurped up the fragrant brew. Not hot by any measure but drinkable.

"It's just that you're so easy to please," she murmured.

He yanked up his gaze. "Hah! Easy to please? Me? As if!" He shook his head, laughing, and went back to sucking up that dark ambrosia. "Then again," he said, pausing, "with you, maybe I am easy to please. Or maybe it's just that *you* please me. I don't really know." What he did know was that he felt absurdly, ridiculously happy.

"And maybe," she said, blushing furiously as she drew her phone from the pocket of her smock, "being gravely wounded has changed your perspective."

He'd give her that. Such experiences were life altering, as he knew only too well. But his wounds weren't what made him glad to be alive for the first time since—he faced the thought squarely—for the first time since he had killed Nick. To his surprise, the pinch of grief and regret did not change the facts.

He was happy. For this moment, he was truly happy.

Suddenly, in a rush of jumbled sensation, he remembered all the other happy moments in his life. The sheer number of them shocked him, things like trying to rope a tumbleweed while his father shouted advice and the west Texas wind blew it first here then there, or crouching low at his mother's side to watch the winding path of a snail in his *oma*'s garden. He felt his father clapping him on the shoulder after a big win, his grandmother's yeasty hugs, his mother ruffling his hair, the dry west Texas breeze and the misting North Sea rain. He could almost close his hand on the satisfying smack of a puck into his mitt, knowing that the net stood empty behind him, and puff his chest with pride as he signed his name to an actual NHL contract. He heard the sound of his own laughter mingled with Nick's and felt his heart trip at the appreciative glance of a pretty girl.

So many happy moments, and somehow they were all embodied in a slight female with big, dark eyes and hair the color of light red sand. Awesome.

By the time Kaylie informed Hilda that he was ready to eat, he had swigged down three-fourths of the coffee and felt the urge to be moving. With her usual careful efficiency, she helped him through his morning routine then wheeled him out into the sitting room and went to get his breakfast from the dumbwaiter.

Stephen found himself talking as he gobbled, his aches and pains easy to ignore. Such was not the case by the time he had cleaned up, changed his clothing and collapsed back onto the bed, even though Kaylie had poked pills down him before-hand. Still, despite the physical complaints, he schooled himself into cheery acceptance when she announced that she must go but would return in time to bring him his lunch.

To his gratification, she seemed to dither about it for a bit, asking, "What will you do with yourself while I'm gone?"

He randomly reached for a book from the stack on his bedside table. "Oh, I'll read, play with my phone, whatever."

"No moving around on your own," she warned. "If you have to get up, call Chester."

Snapping her a smart salute, he squared his shoulders. "Yes, nurse *liefje*."

A smile wiggled her lips. She went out saying, "I'll have Odelia bring you something to drink."

"Juice!" he called out. "Not tea!"

Her laughter was the only promise he got. It was the only one he needed, the only one he wanted, and he'd put up with almost anything to have it. He'd even share her with her greedy father.

Their days took on an easy routine. Aaron popped in and out. On Sunday, he brought his wife with him. Dora was a plump, curvaceous, stylish blonde, with green eyes and a breathless way of speaking that made her seem helpless and none too bright, but in the little time that Kaylie spent with the woman, she learned that the opposite was true. Dora had a witty sense of humor and shrewd judgment. She quickly sized up the situation and voiced her assessment of it.

"Why, Stevie," she breathed, curled up next to her husband on the sofa, "I haven't ever seen you this relaxed."

"Yeah," Aaron joked, "I may need a list of those drugs you're taking."

"It's not the drugs, sugar," Dora corrected, leaning heavily against him. "It's the ambience. Just feel this place." She let her gaze sweep languidly around the room and come to rest on Kaylie, adding, "Of course, I'm sure the company has a lot to do with it."

Kaylie shifted uncomfortably from foot to foot. Still dressed in her Sunday best with her hair held back by a simple headband that left it streaming down her back, she felt like a schoolgirl allowed to sit quietly in a room with the adults—until Stephen smiled up at her and clasped her hand. Suddenly she felt…claimed. And thrilled by it.

Determined to resist such temptations, she quickly made her excuses and escaped to her father. When she returned later, dressed in scrubs, her hair ruthlessly scraped into a bun, it was as if nothing had occurred, and so it remained.

In midweek, Aaron brought one of the team trainers to see Stephen. An earnest, fit, fortyish man with a shaved head, he gave Stephen a careful examination under Kaylie's watchful eye, made some astute observations and asked some penetrating questions.

"You'll be out of that jacket in another few days," he told Stephen, then looked to Aaron. "I'll want to see his X-rays, but if what Miss Chatam says is correct—and I have no reason to doubt her—we may want to tap this Doctor Philem, especially if the facilities down here are adequate."

"Oh, they are," Kaylie was quick to assure him, excited to think that Craig might reap some formal connection with the Blades out of this.

The trainer cocked his head. "We'll see. The situation has some real positives. Buffalo Creek is far enough from the Metroplex to escape some of the harsher scrutiny but still within easy driving distance. Worth looking into."

That's where it was left, until Brooks called on Friday morning to report that the team had asked him to provide a reference for Craig Philem, who was thrilled. He also said that he'd be stopping by as early as possible to check on Stephen. Kaylie was about to head home to prepare her father's lunch when he finally strolled into the sitting room with Odelia on his arm and Chester trailing along behind. Chafing a bit with the inactivity today, Stephen had elected to spend the morning on the sofa with his cast propped on the footstool. He looked up and smiled.

"Hey, Doc! You're just in time for lunch."

"Well, of course, I am," Brooks said. "Exactly as I planned."

"That's not what you told me," Kaylie retorted, folding her arms.

"You're right," he admitted glibly. "I'd hoped to make it in time for breakfast. Lunch is plan B."

Odelia giggled, setting her earlobes to jiggling. Since she was wearing earrings that resembled globs of purple gummy worms, the effect was a little scary. She'd have looked like a walking bait shop if not for the optically disconcerting white spirals printed on her purple cotton sheath, which she wore with white sandals. The wide straps of the sandals and neat, clean lines of the short-sleeved dress lent an odd air of demureness to the otherwise crazy costume. In other words, it was pure, quintessential Odelia.

"In honor of Brooks's visit," she announced gaily, "we're having a garden party." She slipped free of their visitor and went to bend over Stephen, adding, "And Brooks says you may join in, if you feel up to it, Stephen dear. Would you like that?"

"*Tante* Odelia," Stephen said with a grin, "I would love it."

"Are you sure?" Kaylie asked, biting her lip with worry. She couldn't help thinking of the ordeal that the stairs presented.

As if reading her mind, Brooks stepped forward. "I think we can make it a little easier for him." Gently nudging Odelia aside, he began to pull the straps free on Stephen's jacket sling. "For starters, let's get rid of this."

Kaylie helped Brooks carefully maneuver the confining, vest-like object over Stephen's head. Brooks then lifted Stephen's shirt, revealing tautly sculpted muscles, and performed a three-fingered tap along the twin ladders of his ribs. Stephen winced lightly from time to time but never lost his smile.

"Sore but much improved," Brooks pronounced. "Ready to try it without the jacket?"

"Absolutely."

Brooks looked to Kaylie. "Let's get him a simple sling. That'll keep the weight of the cast from stressing his clavicle and shoulder muscles and still let him lift his arm and start moving a little more fluidly."

Stephen eased back on the sofa with an "Aaahhh," and Kaylie smiled, promising, "I'll take care of it this afternoon."

After a few questions and a check of Stephen's pulse and eyes, Brooks stuffed his tools back into the pockets of his suit jacket and offered his arm to Odelia. "I hear Hilda's apple-chicken salad calling me."

She laughed, and they swung toward the door. Chester and Kaylie helped Stephen back into his chair, then the trio started off after Odelia and the good Doctor Leland with Kaylie pushing and Chester again trailing along behind. At the head of the stairs, Stephen rose, balancing his weight on one foot. Kaylie and Odelia went down with the chair while Chester and Brooks took positions on either side of Stephen beneath his arms. Had he been a few inches shorter, they could have carried him. As it was, he hopped lightly from step to step until he reached the bottom and sank once more into the wheelchair.

Odelia hurried ahead, chattering merrily about May Day being the perfect day for a garden party. Stephen tilted his head back, gazing up at Kaylie with wide eyes.

"Good grief. Is this the first day of May? I've lost track."

"It is," Brooks answered for her. Bending low, he murmured to Stephen, "No dancing around the Maypole for you, though."

Kaylie smacked Brooks lightly on the arm with the back of her hand. "Or anyone else, you pagan."

"Hey, I'm an anti-pagan. I firmly believe that Christianity should co-opt every festival and holiday, despite its origins, and make it exclusively our own."

Kaylie couldn't argue with that.

Reaching the end of the east hall, she turned Stephen's chair and backed him down the slight slope into the sunroom. Chester split off and went into the kitchen, while Brooks sprinted ahead to the end of the room near the cozy brick fireplace and opened one side of the French door for Odelia. He threw the other side wide as Kaylie approached with Stephen in the wheelchair. Once more the aunties had rearranged their furniture to accommodate Stephen, a fact he immediately grasped.

"Bright room. Odd furniture groupings." He leaned his head back, smiling. "All for little old me?"

"All for great, massive you," she grunted, shoving his chair over the threshold. He laughed as they gained the outdoors.

The expansive brick patio looked like a spring wonderland, with flowers spilling from a dozen knee-high pots and hanging from graceful wrought-iron stands. The aunties had pushed together two square, redwood tables for their party, creating a space in the center large enough to accommodate Stephen's outstretched leg. The arrangement came with the added benefit of a pair of tall, rainbow-striped umbrellas that rose from holes in the redwood tabletops.

As they reached the table, Stephen sucked in a deep breath, spreading his arms as wide as the cast immobilizing his bent elbow and lower arm allowed. "Now this is my idea of paradise." He nodded toward the figure of a man moving near the greenhouse set back at some distance and asked, "Who's the gardener?"

Everyone looked at Magnolia, who beamed and said, "His name is Garrett Willows. Hired him almost a month ago. Two green thumbs." She turned up her own two in tacit approval.

"Oh, I know him," Kaylie remarked, setting the brake on Stephen's chair. "Or of him, anyway. Isn't he the older brother of Bethany Willows Carter?"

"That's right," Hypatia said, spreading a starched linen

napkin across her lap. As usual, she looked regal in apricot silk, especially next to Magnolia's simple print shirtwaist.

Brooks pulled out the wrought-iron chair beside Stephen for her, and Kaylie absently dropped down into it, musing aloud, "Wasn't there something significant about Garrett?" It hit her suddenly. "Wasn't he sent to—"

Odelia shoved a basket of rolls at her, reaching across Brooks as he took a seat between her and Kaylie. "Have some bread, dear."

"Yes," Magnolia echoed, cutting her eyes meaningfully at Hypatia. "Have some bread."

"Oh, for pity's sake," Hypatia scolded, "as if I don't know the man has been in prison. The two of you act as if I sit in some ivory tower, completely cut off from the rest of the world while you drag in your strays—no offense, Stephen dear. Well, I know what goes on. I remember perfectly that Garrett Willows pled guilty to assault for beating his stepfather half to death."

"Pity he didn't finish the job," Brooks muttered. He cleared his throat when Hypatia shot him a quelling glance. "Sorry. It's just that Garrett went to prison for trying to protect his mother from her husband, and even after that, she stayed with the man. Less than two years later, he killed her."

Kaylie remembered the whole ugly story now, how Bethany herself had used to come to school with bruises and scratches that she'd tried to hide. Garrett had been in his early twenties and Bethany, who was Kaylie's age, about seventeen when he'd taken a baseball bat to their stepfather. Bethany had been newly married when her mother had died, and Kaylie remembered that at the funeral Bethany had sobbed that it was her fault for leaving her mother alone with her brutal stepfather.

Stephen let his gaze sweep around the patio once again in an obvious attempt to lighten the mood. "Don't know this

Garrett, but I'm inclined to believe Magnolia when she says that he has two green thumbs. I suspect that makes four in total."

Magnolia blushed, indicating the level of his success in diverting the conversation. "Why, thank you, Stephen dear." She literally batted her eyelashes at him. Intentionally frumpy Aunt Mags! It was enough to make Kaylie gasp when Aunt Mags cooed, "Are all hockey players so silver-tongued?"

Stephen and Brooks both burst out laughing.

"I think you have me confused with my agent," Stephen said, and that sent Brooks off into a chain of stories about Aaron Doolin's college days that kept everyone at the table laughing merrily for some time.

When Carol placed a plate filled with chicken salad, apple slices, fresh greens and sliced hardboiled egg before Kaylie, she regretfully shook her head. "Oh, no. I can't stay. Dad will be expecting me at home." Checking her watch, she hastily pushed back her chair.

"Nonsense," Hypatia decreed. "Hubner can take one meal alone. We'll make it up to him by inviting him to dinner tomorrow evening. How will that be?" Without waiting for an answer, she looked to Carol, saying, "Bring me a phone, will you, dear?"

"Oh, allow me," Brooks said, pulling his mobile phone from the pocket of his suit jacket and handing it across the table. He shared a conspiratorial smile with Kaylie, who understood perfectly that seeing Brooks's name on the caller ID would add weight to Hypatia's plea.

Kaylie told herself that she should just get up and go, not let the company, food and the beauty of the day seduce her away from her duty. But it was just one meal, after all. Just one. Hypatia made the call, saying that they had coerced Kaylie into staying for lunch because Brooks had arrived and inviting Hub and Kaylie to join the sisters for dinner the following evening. No mention was made of Stephen until Hypatia passed the small phone back to Brooks.

"We'll expect you to join us, too, of course, Stephen dear," she said in an amiable tone that allowed no refusals.

He smiled wryly and inclined his head. "My pleasure."

"And you, as well, Brooks," she went on in a somewhat lighter vein.

He lifted a hand. "Sorry as I am to say it, I have a prior commitment. It's my evening at the free clinic."

"In that case, will you honor us now by praying so that we may eat?"

"Delighted to."

Everyone bowed their heads as Brooks offered simple but eloquent praise and thanks for the company, the surroundings and the meal. Carol reappeared with tall, frosty glasses of iced tea garnished with lemon slices and mint leaves. To Kaylie's surprise, Stephen took a long drink of his.

Lifting his glass, he said, "I've tried telling my friends in the Netherlands that this is how you're supposed to drink tea."

"Hear, hear," Brooks agreed, eliciting a number of politely indignant arguments from the aunts.

Finally, Odelia sat back, smiled indulgently and declared, "Oh, you wretches. You're teasing us!"

Stephen and Brooks just smiled, saying nothing, while the aunts twittered with amusement. Kaylie bit her lip and sent Stephen a laughingly censorial glance from beneath her brow, but he refused to look at her, most likely for fear of giving himself away. One thing she knew about the man was that he could not abide hot tea. Actually, she mused, she'd come to know a good deal more about him than that.

She knew that he could be cross, arrogant and demanding but also thoughtful, sweet and charming. Tough as nails and boyish at the same time, he could display a remarkably selfish nature and then a poignantly needy one as if they were two sides of the same coin. She knew that he was not a believer but that he was respectful enough of her beliefs to discipline his language and behavior so as not to offend. She also knew that his kiss could make her heart explode, his tender touch could curl her toes and his joy could make her positively giddy, all of which seemed to war with the purpose for which God had brought him here, or purposes, as the case might be.

His lifestyle and her own felt at odds, and too many mysteries remained for her comfort, mysteries she increasingly longed to uncover. She thought of this Cherie with whom he was supposedly involved and wondered why she had not put in an appearance by now. Were Stephen her own boyfriend, even if they were just casually dating—and she suspected there was nothing casual about it—Kaylie knew that she would not be so inattentive. She knew, too, that he was a man of whom her father was not likely to approve. Perhaps, she mused, if her father came to know him as she did…

Oh, but what was she doing? Building castles in the air. Forgetting her purpose. Yielding to temptation.

She looked at Stephen, smiling with undisguised delight, and knew that her heart, and perhaps even her faith, was very much at risk.

Chapter Eleven

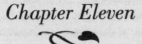

Despite Kaylie's private misgivings, lunch became a relaxed, drawn-out affair. Brooks was the first to leave, but the aunts lingered until the heat, rising into the nineties, drove Hypatia and Odelia indoors. Mags always seemed oblivious to the temperature and trundled off to the greenhouse. Kaylie didn't find the temperature uncomfortable, either, but she was surprised when Stephen suggested that they sit out on a pair of chaises near the fountain.

"Are you sure? It's not too warm for you?"

"No, I love the heat."

"But you spend so much time on the ice."

"Maybe that's why I like it warm the rest of the time. Spending half my life on sixteen-degree ice has given me an appreciation for the other end of the spectrum."

"Sixteen degrees!"

"Yeah, that's why I have to keep moving back there even when the puck's in play on the other end of the court. It's not all that cold, frankly, if you're actually skating. That's why hockey gear is designed to wick away sweat and why I like a little heat."

"All right," she conceded, "we'll stay, but not too long. The last thing you want to do is get a sunburn on top of everything else."

"True."

She pushed him over to the nearest chaise and held the chair while he managed the transfer.

"Ah," he sighed, stretching out. "Most comfortable position I've found in quite a while." He caught her hand as she claimed the second chaise and lifted his face to the sun. "The Dutch love to bask in the sun, you know. Swim, too."

"Really? I thought it was very cool there."

"Most of the time it is, but they do get a little summer, and at the very first sign of it, they hit the water." He chuckled, as if remembering. "It's funny when I think about it. My dad lives out in dusty west Texas where you'd think they'd crave water sports, but the only time I can remember seeing him in a bathing suit he was wearing boots and a cowboy hat."

Kaylie smiled at the mental picture. Curiosity swelled, and she gave in to it, quietly asking, "Why don't you see your father now?"

Stephen blew out a breath through his nostrils. "Well, you have to understand how it was with my parents. Mom was an exchange student at Texas Tech when she met my father. When she got pregnant, he insisted on marrying her or having custody of me. I think he was afraid of exactly what happened, that she'd run back to the Netherlands with me. She was never really happy in the marriage, and she hated west Texas. She and I traveled back and forth between the Netherlands and Texas for years, until we were spending more time there than here. They used to have terrible fights about it. Finally, when I was eight, they divorced. My dad begged me to stay with him, but…"

"She was your mom," Kaylie supplied simply.

Stephen nodded. "They both wanted me, you know? And

that was great, but it was also a kind of burden. I couldn't be with them both at the same time, and Holland was more my home than Lubbock by then. My father and I had almost become strangers."

"He berated you, didn't he?" Kaylie asked gently, indignant on Stephen's behalf. "Called you a mama's boy and a sissy."

"What?" Stephen looked over at her in surprise. "No! Where'd you get that?"

"From what you said in the ambulance." She tried to recall his exact words. "Something about not being a pansy, a mama's boy."

"Oh, that," he said, shrugging dismissively. "That was the best thing my dad ever did for me."

"I don't understand."

"Look," he said, shifting slighting over onto his left side in order to face her, "when I was sixteen I came back to the States to play triple-A hockey. It was my first step toward the pros, and my dad arranged it all for me. He drove to Colorado and convinced a coach there to give me a tryout, flew me over here, hired me a private trainer to get me ready and shelled out a fortune in fees."

"You obviously made the team," she said, and he nodded.

"I did, but it was tough sledding that first year. We practically lived on a bus, playing and practicing in different towns all over Canada and the U.S., but nowhere near Lubbock."

"Not surprising," Kaylie commented.

"More than once I called my dad to come and get me," Stephen went on. "The first time, he did. Drove all the way to Minneapolis. Within a week, I was begging him to take me back. After that, whenever I'd call, he'd, well, he'd say whatever it took to keep me fighting for my spot on that team. Some of those phrases he used became my private mantra. Two years later, I won a full scholarship to college in Wisconsin. From there, I got picked up by the AHL and a year later signed with the Blades. My dad opened the door to all that for me."

"Your father may have opened the door, but you did the hard work," she pointed out.

"True, but I'm not sure I'd have stuck it out if he hadn't egged me on that first year."

"So why the estrangement now?"

Stephen shifted over onto his back again. "It's just that there's always been this distance between us. We haven't spent more than a couple weeks at a time together since I was eight. Then, when I went off to college and he was no longer paying the bills…" Stephen rubbed his forehead, admitting, "It was my fault. Mom didn't like letting me come back to the States, and she expected me to spend my summer and holidays with her, and I wanted to hang with my buddies, you know? Team becomes everything when you're a kid on the road like that. There just didn't seem enough of me to go around, and Dad felt I chose Mom and Nick over him."

"Nick?" Kaylie asked, immediately latching on to that name. It was as if a shutter came down.

"My cousin," Stephen said, sitting up and swinging his legs over the side of the chaise. "Guess it's warmer out here than I thought, and I've got that climb up the stairs to face. We better go in."

"Right. Okay." She got up and brought around the chair. Once he was settled, she pushed him inside. Before they left the sunroom, she stopped. "Let me get Chester." Hurrying through the butler's pantry, she stuck her head inside the kitchen and asked Chester for his help.

It took two trips, one for her and Chester to help get Stephen up the stairs, another for Chester to get the chair up to them.

"We need two chairs," Stephen decided, waiting for Kaylie

to get the sling in place once more. "It's too much work this way. I'll call Aaron."

"Oh, don't bother him with it," Kaylie said. "If you really want a second chair, I'll take care of it."

"Do," he told her. "If you don't have to lug this chair up and down the stairs, I won't feel so guilty for insisting you lug *me* up and down every day from now on."

Kaylie grinned and shared a look with Chester. "I see. Created a monster, have we?"

"Nope. Just gave him a little room to roam. I'd kiss you both for it if I wasn't afraid Chester would break my other arm."

"Good call," Chester quipped blandly, sending Kaylie and Stephen both off into gales of laughter.

They soon calmed down and solved the problem by renting a second chair, a chore accomplished by Stephen himself over the phone. Chester volunteered to go and get it, along with the new sling that Kaylie also ordered, and leave the chair parked in the cloakroom downstairs until needed. This arrangement allowed Stephen a new level of freedom that obviously lifted his spirits and signaled that he was truly on the mend.

Kaylie's own delight was tempered by the knowledge that their time together was growing ever shorter, but she resolutely refused to dwell on tomorrow evening's planned dinner. She would not take hope in it, would not let her imagination flit off on flights of fancy. Her purpose in Stephen's life was to represent Christ to him. His purpose in hers was to help her father regain some perspective on his own life. Anything more would cause a rift between her and her father, and that surely could not be within God's will. Could it?

Later, at home, she brushed off her father's queries about the abruptness of the invitation and even rebuffed a question about Stephen's progress with a bland reminder that she was not allowed to discuss a patient's medical condition.

"Hmm," Hubner said. "Well, I expect I'll be able to judge for myself soon enough. I will be allowed to see him, won't I?"

"Oh, yes," Kaylie replied casually. Why she didn't tell him that Stephen would be joining them for dinner, she didn't know. It may have been the cold, hard weight of dread in the pit of her stomach. Or the hot flutter of guilty hope in her chest.

Stephen felt pretty much as he had the night of his first date—a little sick to his stomach, a little intrigued, a lot hopeful. That first real solo date had come later for him than it did for many young men.

His experiences as a young teen in the Netherlands had revolved around group activities, not that he'd had much time for friends. Hockey had usurped a large portion of his life even back then. After he'd moved to the U.S. to play triple-A at sixteen, he'd had even less time for socializing. It was the summer before college when he'd found himself on the receiving end of a surprising amount of female attention and had finally taken advantage of it.

Or it had taken advantage of him. He'd never been quite sure which. He still remembered that pretty blonde's eagerness and the secret heartache and tawdry disappointment he'd felt when she'd casually moved on to the next guy. He'd kept it light ever since. Concentrating on hockey had seemed the saner course for a lot of reasons. He found nothing light or casual about his feelings for Kaylie Chatam, though—and the two of them were so far from dating that it was sadly laughable.

He looked at himself in the bathroom mirror, critically taking his own measure. Teeth clenched, he smiled and turned his head to check the false teeth filling the upper and lower gaps in the side of his mouth to be sure that they looked natural. Getting one's teeth knocked out was a given in hockey. Cosmetic dentistry loved the sport.

Having managed to shave himself from his chair earlier, with the hand mirror propped against a stack of books, Stephen now tackled his hair with a damp comb and the minimal use of his left hand.

The hair was a problem. He simply had too much of the stuff. It was so thick that he had long ago developed the habit of shaving his head at the beginning of every season and then at the end of it visiting the barber for a good styling, which he kept neat until the beginning of the next season. That way, he didn't have to make time for visits to the barber during the season itself. Several other players used the same system, including a few on his own team. This year, however, the entire Blades lineup had decided, as a gesture of unity, to hit the ice for game one as bald as chicken eggs and not to cut their hair again until the season ended. Like him, they were all looking pretty shaggy about now. He solved his problem by combing the whole mess straight back from his brow and allowing the ends to curl at his nape. That, he decided, tweaking his open collar, would have to do.

Aaron had obligingly driven down that morning with a change of clothing for him, the result being softly pleated, slate-gray trousers and a loose, pearl-gray silk dress shirt that perfectly matched his eyes. With the cuffs left open and rolled back, the sleeves of the shirt were loose enough to accommodate the cast on his arm, but the outside seam of the right leg of his slacks had been carefully split to the knee by Dora. He wore these with dark gray socks and a matching leather belt.

Hobbling back to his chair, a task made surprisingly easier by the absence of the jacket sling, he wondered if anyone would appreciate all the trouble he had gone to in an effort to make himself presentable. Chester said not a word one way or the other as he pushed Stephen to the head of the stairs. Leaving the chair there, they managed the descent, Chester under Stephen's left arm and Stephen supporting himself with his right hand on the stair rail.

He sat in the massive front parlor with the Chatam triplets, flirting shamelessly with all three of them when Kaylie and her father arrived. His heart pounded with ridiculous fervor at the sound of the opening door in the foyer. Two voices called out.

"Sisters?"

"Everyone?"

"In here," Odelia trilled, fluttering her hanky as if they might spy it through the wall. She was dressed this evening all in ruffles, from the creamy pale pink of her soft blouse and skirt to the garish hot-pink of her shoes and earrings. Where she got such outlandish earrings he didn't know, but these resembled quarter-sized leather buttons, each surrounded by a stiff leather ruffle, the whole being the size of a silver dollar.

Kaylie led the way, her step brisk as she entered the room. Her hair, Stephen noted immediately, hung down her back in a straight, silken fall. Only belatedly did he realize that she wore saddle-brown leggings with a sleeveless turquoise-blue tunic, the neckline cut straight across the shoulders. Neat drop earrings, each composed of a single turquoise stone the size of a thumbnail, and simple turquoise-colored flip-flops completed the ensemble, the most fetching, in Stephen's opinion, that he'd seen her wear. He barely had time to take it all in when her father stepped into the room, paused as if to get his bearings and blatantly zoned in on Stephen.

This Chatam was a slender, gangly, pot-bellied older man of medium height with absurdly white, bushy eyebrows and thinning, light brown hair heavily infiltrated with ash-gray. He wore oversized, steel-rimmed glasses, calling attention to penetrating eyes the same dark brown shade as the dress slacks that he wore with heavy black dress shoes, a matching belt and a stark white polo shirt. Stephen nodded in greeting and watched the elder Chatam's sagging face harden around a frown, his shoulders pulling back as those dark eyes took Stephen's measure. The wheelchair, Stephen saw, was dismissed as inconsequential. When a bland expression of dignity smoothed over the older man's frown, Stephen took it as a sure sign that he had been found wanting.

The weight of that felt shockingly heavy. It hurt more than Stephen could have imagined, and given his past that was saying something.

Since Nick's death, Stephen's life had evolved totally around hockey and those who paid attention to such things. When he'd wanted to impress someone, he'd done it on the ice. Unfortunately, Kaylie's father didn't look the sort to be dazzled by a deadly sweeping paddle-down or lightning-fast half-pad butterfly save.

Stephen had known, of course, from the very beginning that money and status counted for nothing here, either. The cachet of old money clung to these Chatams like perfume clung to a rose, though by all appearances Kaylie and her father were of modest means. Judging by the condition and amenities of Chatam House, the old girls themselves controlled a considerable bankroll, but Stephen seriously doubted if any of the three had been shopping for anything more than necessities in decades. In this family, money just did not seem to matter beyond the good that it could do. Otherwise, he would not have donated a handsome sum to some single parents' ministry for the privilege of recuperating within these hallowed walls.

As for status, according to yesterday's table conversation, the Chatams were as apt to take in convicted felons as pro sports figures, which put him in his place quite firmly. Still, Stephen could not complain.

The fact was, these Chatam women were the most generous, caring people he'd ever met. The jury remained out on the men, but with women like these, Stephen couldn't blame the guys if they were more careful and protective than the average father or brother. He even thought that he might be a little offended on behalf of Kaylie and her aunts if such was not the case, all of which meant he had a problem, one he didn't quite know how to handle.

With skill, money and status out of the equation, that just left Stephen with himself, which he knew was sadly lacking.

"Brother!" Odelia gushed, coming to her feet as Kaylie and her father approached. "Come meet our special guest." Hanky fluttering like a bird desperate to escape her plump hand, Odelia made the introductions. "Stephen dear, this is our eldest brother, Hubner Chandler Chatam, Jr."

Stephen resorted to a silent nod by way of acknowledgment, managing to keep perfectly still otherwise. "Hub, this is Stephen." She broke off and turned blinking amber eyes on Stephen. "I'm afraid I don't know your full name, dear."

Leave it to the Chatam sisters to stand on ceremony.

"Oh, um, it's Stephen George Radulf Landeberht Gallow." He made himself smile, though he couldn't remember the last time he'd even spoken his cumbersome moniker.

Odelia beamed. "How delightful!" She turned to her brother. "Hubner, this is—"

"I heard." He thrust his hand at Stephen. A little surprised, Stephen shook it. Sort of. He'd barely begun the motion when Hubner took his hand back, turned and greeted his sisters.

"So how have you all been?" He glanced at his daughter, adding, "Kaylie's brought home surprisingly little news."

The sisters traded looks before putting on their smiles. While Hypatia ably guided the small talk, Odelia and Magnolia doing their parts, Stephen noticed that Kaylie wandered the room, first going to stand by the massive fireplace. She ran her fingertips over the ornate plasterwork before turning away to smell the huge flower arrangement standing atop a tall, three-legged table in the center of the space. From there, she ambled over to a heavy lamp with a colorful stained-glass shade. She was standing by the front window, gazing out over the long, looping drive, when Carol appeared in the doorway to remark that dinner could be served anytime the sisters were ready.

Only then did Kaylie come near Stephen. She walked over to release the brake on his chair and grip the handles in preparation for wheeling him to the dining room. They went last. Hypatia led the way, followed by Magnolia, Hubner and Odelia, in that order. For a moment, it seemed that Odelia and her brother would engage in a mini standoff as each insisted that the other take precedence, but then Hubner sent a pointed glance at Kaylie and went ahead, leaving Odelia to sparkle in their direction, flutter her hanky and prance off after him. Kaylie held a moment longer before backing the chair around and pushing it forward. They had almost reached the doorway when she finally spoke.

Leaning forward, she remarked softly, "You look nice."

Stephen's smile flashed. "You look more than nice."

"Please don't mind my father," she went on anxiously.

Before he could make any sort of reply, she turned the chair into the dining room.

In his opinion, it was the dreariest room in the house. The woodwork had all been stained a black-brown to match the long, rectangular table and towering sideboard. An enormous rug, gold and black figures against an ivory background, did little to break up the darkness. Neither did the dingy wallpaper, yards and yards of it printed with regimented rows of tiny flowers, all seeming to march in lockstep. The only true splash of color in the room came from a bunch of flowers arranged in a long, low crystal epergne with brass feet in the center of the table.

A chair had been removed from the center of the near side of the table, leaving a space between the supporting columns. Odelia needlessly pointed them to it.

"Stephen, you're here, and Kaylie, of course, is beside you."

"Hubner, you can take the head of the table," Hypatia said, giving Stephen the clear impression that this was normally her seat. "I'll sit between you and Stephen." That left Odelia and Hypatia on the other side of the table, with Odelia directly across from him. Smiling at Stephen, she shook out her heavy dark green napkin and spread it across her lap, saying, "I love these intimate family dinners."

Family dinner, he thought, surveying with some amusement the array of dishes and silver in front of him. He wondered hopefully if this made him an honorary member of the Chatam family. Not, he imagined, if Hubner had anything to say about it.

Chester and Carol came in through a door in the end of the room, carrying bowls and platters. Hilda followed with a silver basket of puffy hot rolls. Chester placed a platter of meat surrounded by cooked cabbage directly in front of Hubner, saying, "Your favorite, Pastor Hub."

Hub Chatam rubbed his slightly protruding belly with both hands and looked to Chester's wife. "Hilda, you are a jewel among women." He cast a look at Kaylie, adding, "I haven't had eye-of-the-round roast since I last ate it at this table."

In addition to the beef, cabbage and bread, there were bowls of roasted potatoes, carrots and a dark, rich gravy that had Stephen licking his chops. Without invitation or comment, Hub spoke an elaborate blessing that Stephen frankly had trouble following. The "amens" of the others caught him off guard, causing his own to lag a syllable behind. It was the only word that he spoke of his own accord throughout the entire meal, though the sisters did their best to draw him out with questions and comments. He was polite, of course, and as pleasant as he knew how to be, but Kaylie's careful silence naturally fed his own, while Hubner Chatam's heightened his unease exponentially.

By dinner's end, despite the wonderful food, Stephen longed for the privacy of his sitting room, so when the Chatam sisters suggested that the group gather in the family parlor, Stephen at first declined.

"I—I think I'll just head back upstairs, if you don't mind." He'd have been fine if he'd stopped there, but no, he had to add, "There's an important hockey game on TV that I need to watch."

"Oh!" Odelia squealed. "How lovely! We've been wanting to learn more about the game, haven't we, sisters?"

To his horror, both Magnolia and Hypatia agreed. Desperately, he looked to Kaylie for rescue.

"Are you in pain?" she asked softly. He opened his mouth to lie, but then she checked her watch. "Mmm, not time for your next meds yet."

That's when Hubner Chatam got to his feet and tossed down his napkin, declaring, "Yes, by all means, educate us, if you will, Mr. Gallow."

Caught like a rat in a trap. Kaylie placed a comforting hand on his shoulder, observing softly, "You're going to watch it anyway, and the TV in the family room is larger than the one in your suite."

Sighing inwardly, Stephen put on a smile and nodded.

A mixture of modern furnishings and antiques gave the windowless family room a comfortably casual feel. A pair of overstuffed sofas upholstered in a floral pattern and a trio of comfortable chairs made the space feel homey if a bit crowded. The television was, as promised, a larger version of the one in his suite. At least fifty inches in size, the flat screen hung on the wall adjacent to the obviously well-used fireplace. Under other circumstances, Stephen would have been delighted to watch the game in such surroundings. Unfortunately, watching hockey with the elderly Chatams was every bit as bad as Stephen had feared it would be.

The sisters asked more questions than a roomful of cheeky third-graders, and their brother harrumphed over every answer and explanation. The tactics of the other team didn't improve Stephen's mood any, either. By midway through the second period of play, Stephen was so aggravated that he forgot himself and shouted at the television.

"Come on, ref! How many times are you going to let them interfere with my goalie?"

"*Your* goalie?" Hubner Chatam scoffed. "Why do sports fans always claim a form of ownership? It's not as if you have some actual financial interest in the team, is it?"

Stephen required a moment to fully ingest that seemingly foolish assertion. "Other than the fact that they pay my salary, no, but it's my team, so he's my goalie."

"You *work* for the Blades?" Hubner asked pointedly, his dark eyes going wide behind the lenses of his glasses.

Stephen spread a glance among the women. The sisters seemed as confused as he. Kaylie, however, looked stricken, her cheeks blotched with pink.

"I—I don't guess I ever mentioned that Stephen is the starting goalie for the Blades," she said to her father.

"Was," Stephen corrected, "until I landed here." He smacked the arm of his chair with his palm. Glancing at the TV, he added softly, determinedly, "Won't be in this chair for much longer, though, boys."

Hubner Chatam suddenly catapulted himself to his feet

with much more speed and agility than Stephen would have judged the old fellow capable of. "You're a professional hockey player!"

It sounded oddly like an accusation.

"Yeah," Stephen admitted, his patience beginning to fray. "What's wrong with that?"

The feisty right-winger of the Blades chose that moment to take exception to a cheap shot by an opposition defenseman and dropped his gloves.

"Why'd he do that?" Magnolia asked, pointing to the TV as the two skaters warily circled each other. Abruptly, the players erupted into roundhouse punches.

"Fighting with the gloves on will get you fined," Stephen muttered. "They're hard to protect the hands from flying pucks, so they do too much damage in a scuffle."

"It's all right to fight like this?" Hubner demanded.

"They'll both be penalized," Stephen said offhandedly, "but sometimes it's necessary."

"Necessary!"

"The refs can't be everywhere, see everything. Sometimes the only way to stop something is to let the other team know you're not going to take it anymore."

"It's pointless, barbaric violence!" Hub pronounced. "I've seen enough."

Every head in the room turned to watch him stomp away. He was well out of sight when he bellowed, "Kaylie!"

Moaning, she closed her eyes, but then she rose and hurried after him. At the door, she paused to stammer thanks for the dinner. Then her troubled gaze met Stephen's and she mouthed the words, "I'm sorry."

He could only shake his head. She disappeared, and Stephen reluctantly turned back to the aunts.

Hypatia sighed and lifted her chin. "I apologize, Stephen

dear. My brother's viewpoint has become increasingly narrow in the last few years."

Odelia shrugged and said rather sheepishly, "It is a bit shocking to old ghosts like us, this fighting. Exciting, though."

Magnolia just wanted to know, "Did we win?"

Stephen glanced at the screen. The other team's guy was bloody and headed for the locker room, while the Blades' skater sat in the glass-walled penalty box, grinning.

"Yeah," Stephen said. "Looks like it."

"Good." She nodded decisively.

Less than a minute later, the Blades scored the first goal of the game, and all three aunts cheered with Stephen, though Hypatia was quick to clear her throat, lift her chin and lapse into silent dignity. Too distracted to fully enjoy the moment, Stephen kept one eye on the game and another on the door.

There wasn't much to see in either case. No one scored in the third period, so the game ended with the Blades winning one-zip, and still Kaylie had not returned. The sports commentators lamented the lack of action in this second round opening game, while the aunties clucked over the time and Kaylie's continued absence. Stephen made light of it, suggesting that Chester be called to help him upstairs.

"There's really not much I can't do for myself once I'm back in my room."

It was true. While he ached in half a dozen places, his overall pain had faded to easily manageable levels, and Kaylie had organized his meds so well that he merely had to check the times she had written on those paper cups and toss back the pills. He could pretty well dress and undress himself and lever himself on and off the bed. Managing his meals and getting around would still be a challenge, but he could always call on Aaron or Chester or hire another nurse.

He didn't want to do any of those things, though.

He wanted Kaylie. That he didn't deserve her simply did not matter. His heart wanted Kaylie Chatam.

And he very much feared that tonight had somehow set her forever out of his reach.

Chapter Twelve

Kaylie argued until she was blue in the face—or rather, red—for she had never been so angry with her father. It took every bit of her self-control not to shout at him, for he was being ridiculously unfair.

"It's a sport like any other."

"Sports have their place," Hub said, "but they're not worthy of a grown man's occupation."

"Pro sports are a business."

"What has that got to do with anything? There are many businesses in which I would not want to be involved."

"But that's you. The world does not agree that pro sports is a bad thing."

"The world! Ah, yes, but we are called to stand apart from this world."

"Many Christians, probably *most* Christians, would disagree with you!"

"Fist fighting!" Hub exclaimed, as if that alone explained his objections. "What other sport do you see that in?"

"Football, basketball…"

"Rarely! And never sanctioned. Why, prizefighting is less brutal."

"They clear the benches to fight in baseball," Kaylie pointed out. "Soccer is infamous for brawling."

Hub shook his head stubbornly. "I don't like it! I don't like it because you lied to me, Kaylie."

"I did not! You never asked what—"

"You let me think he was a broken shell, an older man, no temptation."

That last word rocked her because it summed up Stephen Gallow for her perfectly. Temptation. He tempted her to womanhood and affection, to laughter and kisses, to a different life than she had ever imagined and a desperate, hopeful longing. He tempted her to want more for herself than her father wanted for her, and that realization hurt on several levels. He tempted her to love him, to risk even her relationship with her father for that love. It seemed unfair for her father to throw that at her now when she had struggled so to get it right, to do the right thing for everyone, the godly thing. Perhaps she had left out some of the details, but she had done so because she had known that he would overreact. So perhaps she had already dishonored her father. And perhaps that wasn't all her fault.

"I think I had best go before we say things we'll both regret," Kaylie decided softly. "Good night, Dad."

"Kaylie!" he admonished, but for once she ignored him.

She was an adult, after all, fully capable of and fully responsible for managing her own emotions. And she still had a job to do, a job she felt compelled to do. Just how to do it and honor her father, she did not know any longer. She didn't even know what she was supposed to do, what God meant for her to do.

The dilemma became even more confusing when she arrived at Chatam House, let herself in the side door and made her way up the stairs to find Stephen sitting on the edge of his bed in gym shorts and a sleeveless T-shirt, poking around a pill cup. He looked up, seeming unsurprised to see her standing there, and lifted the little paper container, balanced on the tips of the fingers of his left hand.

"This is right, isn't it?"

Nodding, she came forward and took the cup from him, dumping the pills out into his hand. Then she poured him a glass of water from the carafe on the bedside table. He swallowed the pills and set aside the glass.

"Tired?" she asked, noting the shadows about his eyes.

He nodded, but he didn't lie back. Instead, he met her gaze, asking gently, "Has it all changed somehow, Kaylie? I guess I thought we had something going on, something meaningful." He shook his head and asked, "Is that over?"

She folded her arms, feeling chilled and a little lost. They had never spoken of any personal feelings between them, but she wouldn't pretend that such feelings did not exist.

"I don't know. He's my father, Stephen, and my faith teaches me to honor him. I have to consider his opinions, his wishes, his needs, even his fears."

"I don't know what to do. I'm a hockey player, Kaylie. It's all I have, all I am."

"No. No, it isn't. There's more to you than hockey, but I would never ask you to give up hockey just to please my father. That would be like asking you to stop being you, and I'm not sure I could bear that. Unfortunately, Scripture doesn't say to honor your father unless he's completely unreasonable."

"I wouldn't ask you to dishonor him."

"Of course you wouldn't."

Stephen wrinkled his brow. "Isn't there anything I can do?"

She tilted her head. "Pray. We can both pray."

Stephen nodded but was clearly unsatisfied with that answer. "It just seems like there ought to be something more I could do." He reached out with both hands and pulled her to him, the cast on his left palm hard against her waist. "Would it help if I kissed you again?"

"No," she whispered, allowing her regret to imbue her voice, "that would only make it worse."

Gulping, he nodded and put his forehead to hers. "Prayer it is."

She slipped her arms around him. "It's been known to work, you know."

"It's been known not to," he said soberly, pulling back, and then he told her about the night his cousin and best friend, Nick, died.

"I'm that one-in-a-million Dutchman who can't hold his liquor," Stephen admitted wryly, doing his best to keep his resentment at bay. "We drink beer for breakfast in the Netherlands. Oh, not me. Two beers, and I'm done, useless. All my friends know, all my family. Nick used to tease me."

Stephen chuckled softly, hurting right down to the marrow of his bones, but he didn't let that stop him. He told her everything, how he'd sent for Nicklas to come and keep him company in the U.S. They were like brothers, he and Nick, the siblings neither had ever had, his mother's only sister's only child. Just months apart in age, they had practically lived together after Hannah had taken Stephen back to the Netherlands. His aunt Lianna had been like a second mom to him, and it had been the same with Hannah and Nick. So naturally, when Stephen had called, Nicklas had come, and naturally, Nicklas had insisted that a celebration was in order when Stephen formally signed with the Blades.

"A single beer and a glass of champagne was what I had that night," Stephen recalled, "but Nicky, he was tossing them back so fast. We didn't stay long. I preferred to be driving my new car. All that horsepower, all that flash…"

He shook his head and told her what he remembered of the accident, how they'd been fooling around at night on a vacant street in a newly platted neighborhood when a cement truck had suddenly appeared. Stephen had swerved his car out of the way and hit a curb. The car had tumbled downhill over and over until it came to rest on the passenger side, leaving Stephen hanging by the straps of his safety belt above a crumpled and torn Nick.

"I begged," Stephen admitted, closing his eyes. "I begged God not to let him be dead. I begged not to have killed him."

His neck felt stiff, and he rotated his head, trying to loosen the muscles and banish the memories. That was what he'd walked away from the wreck with, a few strained muscles. Nick had died, and he'd had a stiff neck.

He'd been a madman at the site, fighting the emergency personnel, first when they'd tried to treat him and then when they'd taken Nick away. They'd had to sedate him to get him into an ambulance. As a result, there'd been no alcohol test, but the cops had witnesses who'd seen him drinking at the club. Not that it had mattered. Stephen had pled guilty in open court, expecting, almost hoping, for a prison sentence. They'd given him probation, and the team had written a good-conduct rider into his contract.

"So I skate. And Nick's gone," Stephen said, hating the forlorn sound of his own voice. "And I haven't seen my mother, aunt or grandparents since his funeral."

"That's why you don't take your mother's calls, isn't it?"

Stephen hung his head, admitting, "I just can't talk to her without thinking of Nick, without knowing that she is thinking of her only nephew, without knowing that my aunt Lianna will never see her only child again."

"Was Nick wearing a seat belt?"

"No."

"Why not?"

He shook his head. "Because that was Nick—carefree, living on the edge."

"If he'd worn his seat belt he might have survived. You did."

"I was driving," Stephen insisted, "even though I knew I shouldn't have been. They have to know it, too." He closed his eyes. "I don't deserve to have them in my life any longer."

"But they don't deserve to lose you, Stephen. Don't you see? They've lost Nick *and* you."

"I—I can't face them. Nick is gone, and I can't do anything about it. That," he said bleakly, "is how I know prayer doesn't always work."

Kaylie shook her head at him, her hands lightly framing his face. "Stephen, you can't wait until the worst has happened then ask God to undo it."

"Then what's the point?" he demanded. Her hands fell from his face to his shoulders.

"The point of prayer is to keep us in contact with our heavenly Father, to get to know Him. You can't live your life ignoring God and the things of God and then expect Him to offer mercy on demand," she said. "That's like ignoring the law, then when you're caught, expecting the court to come to your rescue. Prayer is as much guidance as rescue, Stephen, and it starts with a personal relationship with God."

"I don't understand. How do you have a personal relationship with someone you never see?"

She folded her arms. "You just told me that you haven't seen your mother in years and go out of your way not to communicate with her, but you still have a personal relationship with her, don't you?"

He shifted uncomfortably, trying to find fault with that logic. "She's my mother."

"And God is your creator."

Stephen gulped. "I—I don't know how *not* to have a personal relationship with my mother, but how do I *start* one with my Maker?"

"You know who Jesus is, don't you?" she asked softly.

"Sure." At least, he'd thought so, until she explained it all to him.

Stephen's gaze turned inward as he considered all that she'd said, and then she gave him the key to his own salvation.

"Don't let your guilt keep you from forgiveness, Stephen. Don't deny yourself the very peace for which Christ Jesus gave Himself on the cross."

They each had too much to think about. By mutual, unspoken assent, they put it all aside when together. Kaylie stole as much time as she could. With Stephen's strength returning and his pain subsiding, she should have been able to leave him on his own more. As long as she left the sling in place on the wheelchair and positioned it properly, he could get himself from the bed and into it and even maneuver himself inch by careful inch into the sitting room. But the suite had become a prison to him, and she knew very well that he lived for the moment when she would help him down the stairs to escape the house.

The rose arbor, accessible from the patio via a bumpy path of paving stones, became their favorite idyll. The arched trellis, weighted with frowsy, bloodred blooms, formed a fragrant tunnel and hid a padded bench inside. Dappled gold sunshine filtered through the leafy shelter, and when the breeze was right, the interior remained cool well into the afternoon. As old-fashioned as it seemed, Kaylie had taken to reading aloud to Stephen, who claimed to be absorbed by the history of explorer Joseph Walker, which she supposedly made even more compelling by her intonation.

While they pretended that their time together was impersonal, so did her father. On a daily basis, he inquired politely, almost icily, how "the patient" fared, and on a daily basis she reported that Stephen was mending well and would soon gain more freedom of movement. That happened on the morning of the fifteenth when Chester brought out the aunts' town car to drive Stephen and Kaylie into town. Stephen had offered to call Aaron to cart him around, but Chester and the aunts would not hear of it. The latter stood waving beneath the porte cochere as they drove away, much like a triune mother sending off a child to the first day of school. Stephen, the big tough guy on skates, waved happily in return through the rear windshield, glad to be going anywhere, even if only to the doctor's office.

Craig Philem greeted them like royalty, and Kaylie couldn't help noticing that most of his approbation was aimed at Stephen this time. Considering that he was now listed among the consulting physicians for the Blades hockey team and busily expanding his office suite to accommodate the honor, she couldn't blame him. He did a most thorough job of x-raying Stephen's broken bones, even those he had not set himself. Pleased, he replaced the initial post-surgery leg cast with a shorter, sturdier version that would allow walking with crutches. To facilitate that, he also shortened the cast on Stephen's upper arm, promising to remove it in another couple of weeks.

They walked out, more or less, side by side, with Stephen swinging lightly on his crutches. Stephen astonished both Kaylie and Chester by insisting upon going shopping.

He bought everything that he could find to fit him at the local men's store, including a suit, though he couldn't even get both arms in the jacket due to the cast. While they waited for the pants to be hemmed, he ambled around the downtown square to pick out gifts for everyone in the house, settling on sunglasses, of all things.

For Odelia he chose gaudy frames ringed in rhinestones, for Hypatia smart pearl-white. Mags wound up with military-green. Chester came away wearing an aviator style, while Hilda and Carol got classic tortoiseshell of different shapes. At Stephen's insistence, Kaylie tried on a dozen pairs or more. In the end, he insisted on a cat-eyed copper frame that cost more than every other pair of sunglasses she'd ever owned. Stephen himself went for a wraparound style in silver with the blackest of lenses.

As a last act of exuberant self-indulgence, he insisted on visiting the local drive-through for milk shakes, ordering one of just about every variety. Later, they all sat around the patio back at Chatam House in their fashionable shades slurping decadently and ruining their lunches, staff included. He was so happy that it hurt Kaylie to think she might actually break his heart. And her own.

She knew what she wanted, but she waited for some sign from God to tell her what she should do.

Stephen felt very proud of himself, at least on one score. He did not attempt to press or seduce or even charm Kaylie. Instead he learned simply to be, with and without her, no artifice or attitude or even thought, taking each moment as it came, living in hope and, oddly enough, praying. The last was harder than he'd thought it would be.

He'd begun simply because she'd asked it of him, but he didn't understand what he was supposed to say to a God whom he did not quite know. In the past, he had made demands or desperate, maddened pleas, but that had not worked out too well, so he did his best just to get acquainted. Telling God about himself, essentially explaining his actions, choices and feelings, seemed foolish. Wasn't God omniscient, all-knowing, all-wise?

Yet, Kaylie had said that prayer must be grounded in a personal relationship with God, so Stephen set about first explaining and then, often, excusing. Or trying to. Funny, but the more he argued his excuses, the less he was able to, and in the process he somehow came to understand himself better. He didn't like everything he found, especially the cowardice and the shame. In fact, some of what he saw in himself brought him to tears and, strangely enough, apology, though he did not quite get why he felt that need. In the end, however, he found a sort of peace with himself. How that could happen, he didn't know, but wanted to. He wanted to understand.

An idea gradually took root, one he'd have scoffed at earlier, and he was trying to find a way to address it when Hypatia did it for him. She made the invitation at dinner on Saturday evening. He had come down for the meal, even though it meant not seeing Kaylie that night. Her father, she had said, required her at home. Stephen didn't like the sound of that, but he couldn't honestly plead a greater need when he was now capable of seeing to himself.

Odelia gushed about how happy they were to see him up and about on his own, and Mags, as he'd taken to calling her, offered to show him around her greenhouse one day early next week. Then Hypatia made her contribution.

"Perhaps, Stephen dear, since you are again ambulatory, you would consider attending church with us tomorrow? It would thrill us to have you there."

He tried to smile and make light of it, as if it were nothing more than taking in a movie or playing a round of golf with his buddies, but the moment felt somber, almost monumental. He couldn't quite pull it off with the necessary insouciance. Instead, he merely nodded and quietly said, "I think I'd like that."

Hypatia patted his hand, Mags beamed; and for a moment he thought Odelia might cry, but then she burst into gay laughter, waved her hanky in the air and all but dived into a particularly sumptuous chicken pot pie.

"You should all know," he said around a bite of that same tasty dish, "that I'm plotting to kidnap Hilda."

The aunts laughed, while he secretly wished that it could be Kaylie, but Kaylie, he had come to realize, would have to be won, and that he could never do on his own, but only by the grace of God.

After dinner the aunts watched the hockey game with him. Ahead two games to one, the Blades lost, allowing their opponent to tie the series. Stephen's disappointment was tempered by the sweet expressions of commiseration that the three old dears heaped on him.

"They'll get 'em next time," Mags offered hopefully, patting his shoulder.

"You'd have beat them!" Odelia insisted, squeezing his face between her hands.

Hypatia merely smiled benignly and advised, "Never doubt that God is in control, Stephen, and working for the benefit of all."

He wanted to believe that with a desperation that frightened him, and that night he besieged heaven from his bed, asking for everything under the sun, from the team winning the Stanley Cup to keeping his position with them, from Kaylie's father's approval to deserving her father's approval, from the strength to win her to the strength to lose her. And finally he found the strength to do something else.

At three o'clock in the morning, he called his mother.

* * *

Daylight found Stephen tired but strangely serene. He dressed himself in the new navy-blue suit pants, a royal-blue shirt and a gray silk tie, black socks and one black shoe. Tossing the jacket over his shoulder, he took up his crutches and made it downstairs in time to share breakfast with the aunties, which they ate at the butcher-block island in the kitchen. As Sunday was a day of rest, the sisters did for themselves, allowing the staff as much freedom from their duties as possible. Chester, however, drove them to church, Hypatia riding in the front seat with him. Mags and Odelia—decked out in bright yellow with huge black buttons, black pumps with yellow bows, a black straw hat with a curled brim and black and yellow beads dangling from her earlobes—rode in back with Stephen. They all sported the latest in sunshades.

To his surprise, Chester, Hilda and Carol all attended church elsewhere, preferring, as Hypatia put it, a less formal evening service. The aunts chose to attend an early one. Chester left them at the main entrance. Odelia fussed over him, helping him into one sleeve of his suit jacket and adjusting the drape of the other side over his cast and sling. He kissed her cheek, and she giggled like a schoolgirl. They walked inside, as strange a quartet as anyone had ever seen, surely, and doffed their sunshades, tucking them into pockets and purses.

A whirlwind of introductions later, Stephen found himself seated at the very front of the soaring whitewashed sanctuary with its oddly elegant gold-and-black wrought-iron touches. The aunties kindly left him on the end of the aisle, with space to stretch out his leg and also for another person or two.

He fought every moment not to turn his head to look for Kaylie, but when another body dropped down onto the pew next to him, he turned with a smile, fully expecting to find her there. Instead, a distinguished-looking, fortyish fellow with medium brown hair and streaks of silver at his temples returned his smile, black eyes twinkling through the lenses of his silver-rimmed glasses. He had a very authoritative air about him, aided by the tan linen vest that he wore with a white shirt, brown suit and red tie. As he possessed the distinctive Chatam cleft chin, it came as no surprise when Odelia leaned close to whisper, "One of our nephews, Kaylie's brother Morgan Charles Chatam."

Before he could take that in, a hand touched his shoulder, and Stephen twisted in his seat to find Kaylie and her father behind him. She beamed as she settled back, but the sour look on Hubner Chatam's face made Stephen's heart sink in his chest. Gulping, he faced forward once more as the small orchestra gathered below the dais began to play. From that moment on, it was a challenge to concentrate, and Stephen found himself, wonder of wonders, falling into silent prayer.

I know I don't deserve her, Lord, or any of the other good things in my life, but I want to. I can't do it on my own, though. No one can truly deserve Your blessing without forgiveness. Isn't that why Your Son took up the cross, that we might be forgiven and forgive in turn? Even ourselves.

With song rising around him, Stephen finally let go of the guilt that had blackened his soul for so long. Afterward, he began to enumerate those good things with which he had undeservedly been blessed. It was a surprisingly lengthy list, not the least of which was the stilted and then progressively cozy talk that he'd had with his mother last night and the three elderly triplets who had opened their home and hearts to him. Somewhere in the midst of it, he got caught up in a prayer being led by someone else, and before he knew what was happening, he was leaning forward to catch every word out of the preacher's mouth.

When the congregation rose for a final hymn, Stephen's mind was racing with all he'd heard and how it supported what he had instinctively learned these past weeks, and then it was over, without him quite being ready. He felt as if he'd been plunked down in a strange place all of a sudden.

This new Chatam, Morgan, stepped out into the aisle and raised a hand to urge Stephen to follow. Without any sort of preliminary, he clapped that same hand on to Stephen's shoulder and addressed him with the familiarity of an old friend.

"Hello, Stephen," he said, his voice deep and resonant, as if it traveled up from a great distance. "Good to see you here. This way." Turning, he led the way up the aisle. Bemused, Stephen slowly followed.

Kaylie fell in beside him as he passed her pew, leaving her father to walk behind with his sisters. "I'm so glad you came," she told him through the brightest of smiles.

For some reason he blurted, "I called my mother last night."

Kaylie gasped and hugged him, nearly knocking him off his crutches. "Oh, Stephen, that's wonderful! How is she? What did she say?"

"She cried," he confessed, "and then she scolded, and then we had a good talk. I promised to visit as soon as I'm able. She's having my houseboat taken out of dry dock for me, in case I decide to spend a few weeks there during the off-season."

"And will you?"

"I think so."

"Oh, Stephen, I'm so proud of you! I knew it. I just knew it. I even told Dad that it would happen."

"You've discussed me, then?"

She wrinkled her nose. "I'm not sure *discuss* is the right word, but yes, we had quite an exchange last night."

Stephen's heart lurched. "And?"

"And," she said gently, "I know God brought us together for a reason. It's in His hands."

Stephen gulped. In God's hands. Nodding, he let her steer him up the aisle, praying that they were moving toward an understanding, a beginning for the two of them. Together.

Chapter Thirteen

Ahead of them, Morgan beckoned, clearing the way through the throng. "Come on, you two," he called loudly, "or we'll never get out of the parking lot."

"I see you've met my brother," Kaylie said, sounding amused.

"I guess you could put it that way," Stephen replied softly. "Does he have to approve of me, too?"

"Oh, Morgan approves of everyone," Kaylie said gaily, "but if you want to impress him, you have to love history."

Stephen sighed.

"I suspect you're talking about me," Morgan said good-naturedly, holding one of a pair of heavy, arched doors open for them. Stephen and Kaylie passed through, and Morgan immediately abandoned the post, staying to Stephen, "I assume sis has told you that I'm a history professor."

"Uh, not exactly."

Morgan clapped him on the shoulder again. Though shorter than Stephen by several inches, he was a solidly built man and packed quite a wallop. "She hasn't exactly told me about you, either, but I'm pretty good at hearing what people don't say." He winked at Kaylie, adding, "I hope you like to eat Mexican. Sis always cooks Mexican when the cowboy comes around."

The cowboy? Thoroughly confused, Stephen watched Kaylie throw her arms around her brother, crying, "Oh, Morgan, I love you!"

"Doesn't everyone?" he chortled, hugging her hard enough to lift her feet from the floor. Releasing her, he slung an arm around Stephen's shoulders. "Now, come on," he said. "Let's see if we can stuff you and that leg into my car."

"But—" Stephen glanced over his shoulder at the aunts, who were just now filing into the foyer with Hubner.

"Oh, no," Morgan declared cheerfully, "they can't help you now." He waved, and Odelia fluttered a black hanky at them. Morgan whirled and started off, the sides of his coat flapping.

"But where are we going?" Stephen asked, struggling to keep up.

"Why, to beard the old lion in his den," Morgan answered, never once looking back.

It was a near thing. Morgan drove a decidedly un-profes-sorial, starlight-blue sports car, and the only way Stephen could get in was to balance on his crutches and slide in legs first, twisting and folding his torso until he was wedged into the seat. Morgan had to open the sunroof and stick the crutches down through the top. Once behind the wheel, he acted like a teenager with a new license, whipping around corners, grinding gears and zipping through tight spaces. Along the way, he explained that things had "come to a head" between father and daughter, and Hubner had "called in re-inforcements," meaning Kaylie's three older brothers, to "help the girl see reason."

"As if," Morgan added, "she's ever seen anything else. I think she's a little too reasonable, if you ask me."

Stephen wasn't sure what that meant or if he even liked Morgan speaking of her that way. "She's just trying to do the best she can by everyone."

"Wouldn't be Kaylie if she didn't," Morgan said. "Brace yourself. We're here, and Bayard has already arrived."

Here was an older white frame house with red roof, red shutters, redbrick wainscoting, detached garage and a tree-shaded front yard. Morgan parked on the street at the curb behind a full-sized, silvery green sedan.

Stephen passed the crutches to him through the sunroof and was still trying to get himself out of the vehicle when Kaylie and Hubner turned into the drive in her boxy little convertible. She rushed to help, Hubner grousing that it surely didn't take both Morgan and her to get Stephen out. It did, though, for he had to come out head and shoulders first, literally crawling his way up and onto his feet and then the crutches.

"I'll get Bayard to take you home in his sedan later," Kaylie promised, walking him up to the dark red door. Hubner and Morgan apparently entered through a back way.

"And Bayard is?" he asked as she opened that door, revealing a small, dark foyer screened from the living area by a wall of carved wood spindles.

"My oldest brother."

She slipped past him, pushing the door wide, but he caught her around the waist, his crutch digging into his already sore armpit.

"Wait. Who's this cowboy you cook Mexican food for?"

"That," said a stern male voice, "would be me."

Stephen looked up at six feet two inches of boots, snug jeans and well-filled-out chambray shirt. His big, thick hands parked at his waist, the cowboy in question lifted a heavy, sandy brown eyebrow, silently challenging Stephen's right to so much as touch Kaylie. Stephen looked at that hard, set face with its dimpled chin and knew he'd finally met his match. All right, he thought, resisting the urge to toss aside his crutches, let the battle begin.

"Chandler!" Kaylie cried, launching herself.

"Hey, sprite!" Catching her up, Chan spun her around before setting her feet to the floor again—as far away from Stephen as possible. Stephen frowned at that.

"I didn't see your truck."

"It's got a four-horse trailer hitched to it, so I had Kreger drop me."

"Kreger is Chandler's partner," Kaylie explained to Stephen, "both in a ranch outside of town and the rodeo arena, where they compete in team roping, among other events." She turned back to her brother. "Are you in town for long?"

He eyed Stephen and rumbled, "Long as it takes."

Stephen smiled and said conversationally, "You know, I'm not as helpless as I look."

"Oh, stop," Kaylie admonished, stepping to Stephen's side and sliding an arm across his back to urge him forward. "This isn't a macho-man contest. Behave yourselves, both of you. Come in, Stephen, and sit down."

Smugly, Stephen allowed her to direct him past Chandler and a dark hallway into a surprisingly large, oak-paneled living room with an impressive rock fireplace. Cushions had been scattered across the knee-high hearth, and it was there that Stephen chose to sit, craning his neck to view the portrait over the mantel. An oil painting of a sweet-faced woman, it had to be Kaylie's mother, given the red hair, bobbed at chin length, and big brown eyes.

Across the room, in front of a sliding glass door that looked out onto a wild, pretty garden, Kaylie's father somberly occupied a brown corduroy recliner, and another man took up one end of a long, matching sofa with an enormous rectangular coffee table parked in front of it. Rather portly with thick lips and a deeply cleft chin, he had stuffed his big belly into an expensive, black three-piece suit and looked like the sort who might sleep in silk ties, so much a part of his daily routine were they. His brown eyes goggled when he saw Stephen.

"Good grief!" he exclaimed. "You're Hangman Gallow. I heard they signed you at three million a year."

"It's not straight salary," Stephen said somewhat defensively. Indeed, once the taxes, annuities and expenses were paid it amounted to much less, but even that figure was ample.

"No, no, of course not," the other man said. "Wouldn't be wise. I'd be glad to look at the structuring of it for you."

"This is my oldest brother, Bayard," Kaylie put in, her smile a tad strained. "He's a banker."

"This is not a business meeting!" Hubner declared hotly.

"No one said it was," Bayard retorted, "but a good businessman always has his eyes and ears open."

"Well, there you have it," Morgan said cheerfully, strolling over to lean with both hands on the back of the sofa. "Bayard votes for Stephen's bank statement. I vote for Kaylie's good sense, and Dad and Chandler, while forever at odds over everything else, especially Chandler's chosen profession, vote for their own convenience."

"I resent that," Chandler snapped.

At the same time, Hubner declared, "The Chatam men have always prided themselves on their decency and refinement. We are bred to boardrooms and pulpits. We put our skills and educations to the betterment of others, not frivolous, barbaric sport! We are ministers and, yes, bankers, professors and lawyers—"

"Shipping magnates and doctors," Chandler went on in a bored voice, "apothecaries and the odd state senator, authors and orators and scientists… Yes, I know, anything but professional cowboys."

"Or hockey players," Stephen muttered.

As one, Chandler and his father turned on Stephen, barking, "You stay out of this!"

"Chatams are good Christian men," Hubner went on, "who embrace their God-given responsibilities with faith and obedience. They are—"

"I believe the word you're looking for is 'snobs,'" Chandler sneered.

"No such thing!" Hubner pounded the arm of his chair. "A Christian man is humble! He doesn't need to beat another, only to do his best in the eyes of God! He is no brute!"

"Was King David a brute when he slew Goliath?" Chandler demanded. "Was Gideon a brute when he led God's army? Was Joshua—"

"What is going on?" Stephen roared, effectively silencing the room, so effectively that he was a little embarrassed. "You didn't bring me here to watch a family feud," he added sullenly.

"I didn't bring you here at all," Hub grumbled.

"That was me," Morgan admitted cheerily. "Only seems reasonable if sis is going to marry him."

Startled, Stephen swung his gaze to Kaylie, who stood in the center of the room, twisting her hands together. Her face colored, and she wouldn't look at him, but he could have cried for joy. He'd always known that with Kaylie Chatam it would be marriage or nothing. He couldn't bear the thought of nothing, but he'd hardly dared hope for anything else.

"I didn't say I was going to marry him," she refuted smartly. "I only said that I'd marry him if he asked me to."

"He will," Stephen said flatly. "He is." He glared at Chandler when he said it, but the big cowboy was looking poleaxed.

"Sugar, are you sure about this?" Chandler asked, moving forward to cup Kaylie's elbows in his big hands. "He's a hockey player. That's a different world."

"I'm not from Mars," Stephen said dryly. "My father's a rancher in west Texas. Mom's a fashion designer in Amsterdam. My stepfather's a flower broker."

"Flower broker!" Chandler yelped.

"It's big business over there," Bayard put in helpfully. "Largest flower market in the world."

"Well, there you have it," Morgan pronounced. "Big business and big money with a side order of west Texas thrown in. What else could you want?" He wagged his finger at no one in particular, adding, "And you said I shouldn't have brought him along."

"You didn't bring him here," Kaylie said, moving to Stephen's side and sliding her arm across his shoulders. He carefully let out a breath that he hadn't even realized he'd been holding and reached up to grasp her hand. "Not really. God did. I'm convinced of it."

Stephen closed his eyes. *Thank You, Lord.*

"You believe that because you want to believe it," Hub said desperately.

"Yes," Kaylie gently replied, "and you won't believe it because you don't want to, but I love him, and I believe God means us to be together, and that's all there is to it."

"You love me?" Stephen said, as near tears as he could possibly be without sobbing.

"Of course I do."

"And I love you," Stephen hastily supplied, laughing with relief as moisture gathered in the corners of his eyes. He reached across with his right arm, wrapped it around her waist and pulled her down onto his lap. Kaylie's soft smile launched his heart into a whole new stratosphere of delight.

"But what about Dad?" Bayard was demanding.

"If you marry, he'll be alone," Chandler said worriedly to Kaylie.

"I'm alone, Chan," Morgan pointed out, "and so are you. Bay's the only one of us who has his own family."

"But Dad's health—" Chandler began.

"Is better than most men's his age," Kaylie said gently.

Hubner cast a look at that portrait over the mantel, grimaced and turned away. In that moment, Stephen understood a large part of the problem. It was fear, the fear of loneliness and change, but the solution was so simple that he didn't understand why they couldn't all see it.

"Who says he has to live alone?"

"I won't have a babysitter!" Hub declared bitterly. "And I won't be forced into one of those smelly warehouses." He visibly shuddered at the thought. "I won't be foisted onto my sisters, either. They're almost as old as I am, and they sacrificed enough of their lives taking care of our father."

"But you'd have Kaylie do the same thing," Morgan pointed out.

Hubner blanched, muttering, "It's not the same thing. Kaylie has a calling."

"To nursing," Kaylie said, "not to singlehood. The aunts are called to singleness, Dad. I am not."

"You're missing the point," Stephen said, tugging on Kaylie's hand. He smiled up at her, saying, "I have no objection to Mr. Chatam living with us."

Kaylie gasped. "Stephen!"

"I'll take you any way I can get you, sweetheart. Aunts, brothers, fathers, the whole kit and kaboodle, whatever it takes. Besides," he whispered into her ear, "I have a really big house."

She wrapped her arms around him. "Stephen."

Across the room, Hubner Chatam's eyes had widened behind his glasses. "I—I couldn't leave Buffalo Creek," he sputtered, but Stephen detected a note of hopefulness in his voice.

"Why not?" Morgan asked. "Bayard has."

Bayard humphed. "It's a business decision. The bank's in Dallas, but Buffalo Creek is still home."

"Uncle Murdock did and Aunt Dorinda," Morgan went on. "I can name you a dozen others."

"I am not the others," Hub snapped. "I am the eldest Chatam, and the Chatams are Buffalo Creek. We have a responsibility to this town. Buffalo Creek is my home. My..." He paused then finished softly, "My ministry is here."

"Was here," Morgan said gently, "until you abandoned it."

"I didn't abandon it," Hub argued. "Chatams do not abandon their callings." He put a hand to his head. "It abandoned me really, though I prayed that God would take me before that happened."

"Oh, Dad," Kaylie said. "Why don't you see that God still has use for you? Why else would he let you recover so well from your heart attack? And just think what that experience could mean to others in the same condition."

He glanced around guiltily. "Who would listen to an old man whose best days are behind him?"

"I would," Stephen said. "In fact, I—I have some questions that I need answered, if you don't mind. Spiritual questions. Who better to ask than you?"

Hub's eyes went very wide behind his glasses. After a moment, he cleared his throat. "I'm sure we'll have some time to talk after lunch," he muttered.

Kaylie smiled at that and laid her head on Stephen's shoulder. "Thank You," she whispered. "Oh, thank You. Thank You."

Stephen did not assume that she was thanking him, but he would give her all the reason to do so that he could.

"As for leaving Buffalo Creek," he said brightly, "I like it here. No reason we can't find or build a house nearby."

"Not the Netherlands?" Hub asked.

"Kind of a long commute to Fort Worth," Stephen said.

"The Netherlands is for vacations. And honeymoons?" he whispered into Kaylie's ear. She tightened her arm around his neck, so he added, "For starters. After that, I was thinking Italy."

"And when were you thinking of taking this honeymoon?" she whispered back.

"I've always wanted to be a June bride," he muttered, and she giggled.

"All right, enough of that," Chandler ordered.

"Not from where I'm sitting," Stephen retorted cheekily.

"Time enough for it later, then," Bayard said, hoisting himself to the edge of the sofa. "When do we eat? I'm starved."

That did it. Smiling broadly, Kaylie popped up and rushed toward the kitchen. "Morgan, add a plate to the table. Chandler, that salsa you like is in the refrigerator. Bayard, you'll have to sweeten the tea yourself. Stephen…"

He grabbed his crutches and got to his feet. "Yes?"

She whirled around, smiling dreamily. "Just…Stephen." With that she danced away, her brothers following. That left him alone with his future father-in-law, who got up and walked to his side. Stephen waited, and after a moment Hub spoke.

"I can't approve of your occupation."

Stephen quoted from that morning's sermon. "'Seek not the approval of man but the approval of Him Who is above man, of God Himself.' I think that's what the pastor said."

Hubner cleared his throat. "Yes, well, I expect you'll grow on me."

Stephen chuckled. "I expect I will."

"Is that so?"

Stephen nodded. "Kaylie's spoken to me about a personal relationship with God through Jesus Christ. I figured you would be the one to explain that to me."

"I—" Hubner's chin wobbled and his face softened. "Yes," he said, thawing, "I would be the one." He cleared his throat again. Sucking in a deep breath, he admitted, "I fear there are some things I need to get off my chest first."

"I've been doing some of that myself," Stephen told him. "Comforting process."

"Yes," Hubner agreed, clapping him on the shoulder and starting him toward the dining room. "Yes, it is. Maybe you can, ah, give me a better understanding of hockey later. One should have all the facts, after all."

"Be glad to," Stephen said. "Lately I'm all about promoting understanding in the family."

"Family," Hubner echoed, bowing his head. "I may be too proud of mine," he admitted.

"Well," Stephen allowed, "it seems to me that you have plenty to be proud of." He glanced over his shoulder at the painting above the mantel. "Beautiful woman, Kaylic's mother."

Hubner's gaze followed his. "Yes, she was."

"Almost as beautiful as her daughter."

Hubner smiled. It was reluctant. It was wan. It was the first sure sign of peace between them but not, Stephen felt sure, the last.

Chapter Fourteen

"**S**tevie baby!"

Stephen and Kaylie twisted in their seats to wave at Aaron and Dora Doolin.

They weren't the first unexpected guests to stop by the VIP arena box that night. The infamous Cherie and a small coterie of seductively clad "ice bunnies" had flounced in earlier—and then right out again upon Stephen's formal announcement of their engagement. Stephen had seemed sheepishly amused. Kaylie had looked at the ring on her finger and smiled to herself, confident in her beloved and the God Who had brought him to her.

Beaming megawatt smiles, the Doolins plunged into the milling throng of Chatams, paramedics and friends helping themselves to the buffet provided by the arena caterer. Beside Stephen and Kaylie, the aunts, too, greeted the newcomers. Odelia, decked out in the team colors of maroon and yellow-gold, waved her hanky at them, the garish walnut-sized garnets on her earlobes sparkling like disco balls. Hypatia, in pearls and pumps, granted them a regal nod, but Aunt Mags, dowdy as ever, barely glanced their way before turning back to the action on the rink, if the Zamboni reconditioning the ice could be called action.

After two periods, the Blades were trailing in the make-it-or-break-it seventh game of the series, but Stephen seemed to have recently turned philosophical about the outcome and his part in it. Or lack of part in it, if the team so decided. He was through hiding like a guilty child, he'd said. A soon-to-be-married man had to learn to face his failures and responsibilities—and leave the rest to God.

For that reason, he'd met with team management and explained himself as fully as possible, vowing never to drink again. He had also invited his father here tonight, at Kaylie's urging. George Gallow hadn't even replied, but at least, Kaylie told herself, Stephen had made the effort. She was terribly proud of him.

Aaron made his way to the front of the box, towing Dora behind. When they reached the double row of seats overlooking the ice, however, it was Dora who spoke first.

"Lemme see! Lemme see!" Grabbing Kaylie's hand from Stephen's, she gasped at the elegantly simple two-carat, marquis-cut diamond on Kaylie's dainty finger. "Ooh, classic. I'm so happy for you." She smacked Stephen on the cheek, adding, "I'm happier for you."

"Thanks." He and Aaron shook hands, Stephen saying, "I thought you were hobnobbing with team management tonight."

"Oh, yeah, and brother are you going to be happy when you hear my news." Aaron bounced on the pads of his feet.

"What news?"

Aaron leaned close and muttered in a voice audible by everyone in the suite, "Kapimsky's going to Canada."

"No kidding!"

"They're rebuilding up there and need a hotshot young goalie to get 'em into the playoffs." He pounded Stephen on the shoulder and, grinning, added, "They wanted you, but the team won't let you go."

Stephen closed his eyes, hugging Kaylie tight with his right arm. Stephen sighed as if a weight had lifted from his shoulders. He brought his hand around and clapped palms with Aaron. "Thanks, man. That's a great wedding present."

"Speaking of presents, the team's got something for you. Will you come down to the locker room right after the game and bring the better half with you?"

Stephen uneasily shifted in his seat, his cast knocking against the half wall at the edge of the box. "I don't know. It would mean running the press gauntlet, and Kaylie may not be ready for that."

"We'll be there," she said confidently, and Stephen's arm tightened.

"Thanks, babe," he whispered.

Half an hour later, it was all over. The team had lost by a single point, their opponents advancing on to the finals, but no one could expect them to hang their heads. They'd come a long way fast, and the future looked bright. Kaylie and Stephen rose to make their way downstairs, taking their leave of the family with kisses and pats and handclasps.

Hubner came over to squeeze Stephen's shoulder and say, "Next year, son. Next year."

Smiling, Stephen nodded. Kaylie knew that her father would never be a hockey fan, but he showed signs of becoming a Stephen fan, and that was what counted most.

Aaron returned to run interference for the happy couple, keeping the press from eating them alive and checking the locker room to make sure that everyone was still decent before ushering them inside. Stephen paused, his weight balanced on his crutches. Kaylie's slipped her hand supportively into the curve of his elbow. Instantly, they were swamped by sweaty skaters speaking half a dozen different languages. The team captain called for order and got it.

"These are yours, man," he said to Stephen, producing three battered pucks. "One for every game we won in this series."

Stephen shook his head. "No, I can't. Kapimsky should get those. He—"

Kapimsky stepped forward. "You got us here, dude, and you gave me my shot. Those pucks are yours."

Kaylie beamed as the two shook hands, and Stephen congratulated Kapimsky on his new contract.

"Next year, all the way!" someone called.

A cheer went up. After it died down, Stephen made introductions. The men congratulated him and joked with Kaylie about being the team nurse.

"Well, I have specialized in pediatrics," she quipped. "That ought to qualify me for the position."

Stephen laughed with everyone else. They stayed a few moments longer, then got out so the guys could strip and shower. Monday morning, Stephen said, they'd start cleaning out their lockers, the season finally having come to a close. He seemed at peace with that.

Aaron pocketed his phone, saying, "I called your car around. Head on out back. They'll be waiting for you."

Stephen had hired a series of limos to ferry the family to and from the game so no one would have to worry about getting lost or finding a decent parking place. He passed the hockey pucks to Kaylie, saying, "Can you hold these for me, babe?"

She dropped them into her purse. "I can't imagine they'll be the only ones."

"Let's hope not!" Aaron quipped. "I'll pick them up later and get them into the display case."

The case had been moved to Aaron's office for safekeeping while Stephen's Fort Worth house was being repaired and put on the market. He and Kaylie, meanwhile, had an appointment with an architect for the following week and were already shopping for a small acreage near Buffalo Creek to build on, as well as a house to rent in the meanwhile.

By the time they reached the car, she could tell that Stephen was tired but pleased. He stood back to let Kaylie slide into the long black vehicle through the door held open by the driver, but a voice from the shadows near the arena stopped her.

"Steve."

He turned so quickly that he almost fell. Kaylie's hand flashed out to steady him, but it was another that set him to rights, a big square hand thickened with maturity and hard work.

"Dad!"

George Gallow backed away a step. Shadows carved hollows in the cheeks and eye sockets beneath the hat that he wore, but the resemblance to his son was marked. Tall and lanky with feet and hands the size of small boats, he was a large, vibrant, if quiet, presence.

"I didn't think you'd be here!" Stephen exclaimed. "Why didn't you come up to the suite?"

George shrugged. "You know me, not much for crowds."

Kaylie moved up close to Stephen. He reached back for her, pulling her forward.

"So this is the one, huh?" George said.

"This is the one," Stephen confirmed.

George swept off his hat, smoothed his dark blond hair with his hand and nodded. "Pleased to meet you."

Impulsively, Kaylie stepped up and hugged him. "It's a pleasure to meet you, too. Thank you for coming."

He didn't lift a hand to return the embrace, but he didn't back away, either. "Mmm," he said, "not the first time. Don't s'pose it'll be the last."

"You've been here before?" Stephen asked, clearly shocked.

"Time or two."

"Why didn't you let me know?"

"Wasn't sure you wanted to see me."

"Dad," Stephen said, sounding exasperated, "I've always wanted to see you. I just… I didn't know how…"

George Gallow nodded his understanding. "Okay. It's okay, son."

"I haven't done a very good job of letting you in, have I? I'm sorry for that."

George Gallow shrugged, standing awkwardly, and Stephen did what Kaylie prayed he would. He hobbled forward and wrapped his arm around his father's shoulders. George caught his breath and pushed it out again, then he patted Stephen on the back before quickly pulling away.

"Guess I'll see you at the wedding then."

"Well, I'll be there," Stephen quipped.

George Gallow grinned. "Me, too." He ducked his head, adding, "Better let your mother know."

"Don't worry about that," Stephen said, smiling. "It'll be fine. From now on, everything is going to be just fine."

"Be a nice change," George said, fitting his hat back onto his head. Then he nodded at Kaylie and walked away.

"Well," Kaylie said, laughing.

"Very well," Stephen said, slipping his arm around her waist. "Extremely well."

"I wish it could have worked out for them," Kaylie said with a sigh, "your mom and dad, I mean."

"I know," Stephen said. "I do, too, but they were never a good match. Not like us."

"A Dutch hockey player and a pediatric nurse," she reminded him pertly. "Not many would put us together, I imagine."

"A half-Dutch, half-Texan hockey player."

"It's still a weird match," she teased, leaning into him. "A match that could be made only in Texas."

He laughed and folded her close. "Or heaven."

So it was. A match made in Texas. And heaven.

He laid his cheek atop her head, and she closed her eyes. Silently they praised God. Together.

* * * * *

Dear Reader,

As Christians, we want to believe that as long as we are obedient, prayerful and seeking to serve God, our lives should be smooth and without problems, but here in this world, bad things happen even to "good" people, and sometimes we are overwhelmed by them. So what is the point? Why would God create this world and place us in it?

I believe that it's primarily a matter of us learning to love Him, and the love that builds our families is surely a part of that. What better demonstrates our relationship to our Lord than a wise parent or obedient child? Or a not-so-wise parent and disobedient child?

It seems to me that our job is simply this: to love.

And so, may you love. Always.

God bless,

Arlene James

QUESTIONS FOR DISCUSSION

1. Kaylie believes that the Ten Commandments apply to Christians today. How seriously do you think most Christians take them? Why should Christians take them seriously? Why not?

2. Kaylie interprets the commandment to honor her father as taking into consideration his opinions, feelings, fears, wishes and convictions. Is that the meaning of the verse? If not, what is?

3. After her mother's death, Kaylie's father leaned on Kaylie for support. Do you think he goes too far? How could she have tried to get him to be more independent sooner?

4. Hubner holds some fairly controversial opinions, especially in a culture that admires professional athletes. Do you agree or disagree with his conviction that professional sports are frivolous and unworthy? Why or why not?

5. Hubner seems to have lost his way in the latter years of his life. Is that possible for a Christian minister? Why or why not?

6. Stephen has carried a great deal of guilt over past mistakes. Acts 10:43 says, "All the prophets testify about Him that everyone who believes in Him receives forgiveness of sins through His name." How would this be of service to Stephen?

7. Stephen's guilt seems to have led him to anger. At whom might Stephen be angry? God? Himself? Nicklas? How did this guilty anger impact Stephen's life?

8. Stephen led a life in the fast lane, which came to a crashing halt, literally. Do you think Stephen's car crash was exactly what he needed to get his life back on track? Why or why not?

9. Since his cousin passed away, Stephen isolated himself from his mother and the rest of his family. Was this the right thing to do? How could his family have helped him through his grief?

10. Christians speak of those who are called to ministry. Are Christians called to such other occupations as the law, banking, teaching, nursing, sports? Are there any occupations to which Christians are not called? Why or why not?

11. The Chatam sisters have remained unmarried throughout their lives. Hubner believes that they have been called to singlehood. Are people ever truly called to singlehood? Why or why not?

12. Being in such close quarters together, Stephen and Kaylie grew to care for each other in a short period of time. Has this ever happened to you with someone? What was the result?

13. Do you think it was the Chatam sisters' intention all along to match up Kaylie and Stephen? Why or why not? Do you know any people who like to matchmake? Have they been successful?

Read on for a sneak preview of
KATIE'S REDEMPTION
by Patricia Davids,
the first book in the heartwarming new
BRIDES OF AMISH COUNTRY *series,*
available in March 2010
from Steeple Hill Love Inspired.

When a pregnant, formerly Amish woman
returns to her brother's house, seeking forgiveness
and a place to give birth to her child,
what she finds there isn't what she expected.

Please, God, don't let them send me away.

To give her child a home Katie Lantz would endure the angry tirade she expected from her brother. Through it all Malachi wouldn't be able to hide the gloating in his voice.

An unexpected tightening across her stomach made Katie suck in a quick breath. She'd been up since dawn, riding for hours on the jolting bus.

Her stomach tightened again. The pain deepened. Something wasn't right. This was more than fatigue. It was labor.

Breathing hard, she peered through the blowing snow. It wasn't much farther to her brother's farm. Closing her eyes, she gathered her strength.

One foot in front of the other. The only way to finish a journey is to start it.

She sagged with relief when her hand closed over the railing. She was home.

Home. The word echoed inside her mind, bringing with it unhappy memories that pushed aside her relief. Raising her fist, she knocked at the front door. Then she bowed her head and closed her eyes, grasping the collar of her coat to keep the chill at bay.

When the door finally opened, she looked up to meet her brother's gaze.

Katie sucked in a breath and then took a half step back. A tall, broad-shouldered Amish man stood in front of her with a kerosene lamp in his hand and a faintly puzzled expression on his handsome face.

It wasn't Malachi.

To read more of Katie's story,
pick up KATIE'S REDEMPTION
by Patricia Davids,
available March 2010.

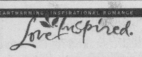

LARGER-PRINT BOOKS!

GET 2 FREE
LARGER-PRINT NOVELS
PLUS 2 FREE
MYSTERY GIFTS

Love Inspired®

Larger-print novels are now available...

LILP10